*"You have a reputation...
children's spec...
turned your ba...*

"You don't have an...

"I don't have to." Gavin held up a hand. "I'm a father. I'd slay dragons and storm fortresses if it would make my son the way he was. I can't help him, but you can."

"Not anymore."

"I don't buy that. You got positive results in the past. Why not now?"

"I don't owe you an explanation."

"No. That's true. But the fact is I'm not giving up until I get one."

M.J. recognized the determination on his dark features. "An explanation? It's called survival, Mr. Spencer. I simply can't get wrapped up in a child. I can't do it anymore."

"Why?"

"I don't have the heart. My son took it with him when he died."

Dear Reader,

I'm not a math person at all. Language and reading skills have always been my strengths. When a wonderful book goes from my to-be-read stack to the "keeper" shelf, I'm grateful to a teacher.

The idea for *At the Millionaire's Request* came to me while I was out to dinner with two friends who happen to be teachers. Connie and Marilyn can't go anywhere without running into former students or parents of former students. That night a couple stopped by our table and said they'd taken care of our bill, which naturally made me curious.

It turned out their son had suffered a traumatic brain injury and Marilyn had tutored him in addition to her demanding job as a kindergarten teacher. This mom and dad were incredibly grateful for her dedication and one-on-one work with their child. Reading is automatic for me and I take it for granted. But that incident made me realize the phrase, "I touch the world, I teach" isn't just words.

When I read a book, a magazine or write a romance novel, I'm grateful to my teachers. Speech-language pathologists take learning to a different and more challenging level and have my profound respect.

At the Millionaire's Request has been a project dear to my heart. I hope when you read the story it touches yours, too.

All the best,

Teresa Southwick

AT THE MILLIONAIRE'S REQUEST

TERESA SOUTHWICK

SPECIAL EDITION®

Published by Silhouette Books

America's Publisher of Contemporary Romance

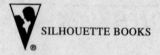 SILHOUETTE BOOKS

ISBN-13: 978-0-373-24769-1
ISBN-10:   0-373-24769-9

AT THE MILLIONAIRE'S REQUEST

This edition published by arrangement with Harlequin Books S.A.

® and TM are trademarks of Harlequin Books S.A., used under license.
Trademarks indicated with ® are registered in the United States Patent
and Trademark Office, the Canadian Trade Marks Office and in other
countries.

Visit Silhouette Books at www.eHarlequin.com

Printed in U.S.A.

Books by Teresa Southwick

Silhouette Special Edition

The Summer House #1510
  "Courting Cassandra"
*Midnight, Moonlight &
  Miracles* #1517
It Takes Three #1631
The Beauty Queen's Makeover #1699
At the Millionaire's Request #1769

Silhouette Romance

*Wedding Rings and
  Baby Things* #1209
The Bachelor's Baby #1233
A Vow, a Ring, a Baby Swing #1349
The Way to a Cowboy's Heart #1383
And Then He Kissed Me #1405
With a Little T.L.C. #1421
The Acquired Bride #1474
Secret Ingredient: Love #1495
The Last Marchetti Bachelor #1513
**Crazy for Lovin' You* #1529
**This Kiss* #1541
**If You Don't Know by Now* #1560
**What If We Fall in Love?* #1572
Sky Full of Promise #1624
†*To Catch a Sheik* #1674
†*To Kiss a Sheik* #1686
†*To Wed a Sheik* #1696

Silhouette Books

*The Fortunes of Texas:
  Shotgun Vows*

††*Baby, Oh Baby* #1704
††*Flirting with the Boss* #1708
††*An Heiress on His
  Doorstep* #1712
§*That Touch of Pink* #1799
§*In Good Company* #1807
§*Something's Gotta Give* #1815

*The Marchetti Family
**Destiny, Texas
†Desert Brides
††If Wishes Were…
§Buy-a-Guy

TERESA SOUTHWICK

lives with her husband in Las Vegas, the city that reinvents itself every day. An avid fan of romance novels, she is delighted to be living out her dream of writing for Silhouette Books.

To speech-language pathologist Christine Rosenthal
who patiently and in great detail answered all my
questions about what she does.

To my friend and middle school teacher, Connie Howard,
who reminded me that her niece Christine is an SLP.

To my friend and kindergarten teacher,
Marilyn Tobin, who was at dinner with
Connie and me when grateful parents stopped
to thank her for her dedication to their son.

The encounter inspired this book. The three of you are
an inspiration to me and all your students in spite
of the way it sometimes feels.

Teachers rock!

Chapter One

Gavin Spencer would make a deal with the devil if it would help his son.

And this just might be hell, he thought, staring at the high school kid with his red-tipped, spiked Mohawk and so many piercings it looked like he'd fallen face-first into a tackle box.

"In the office they said I could find M. J. Taylor here," he said to the teen sprawled in a student desk.

"Who?"

"Your teacher."

"You mean, the sub?"

"If M. J. Taylor is your substitute teacher, then yes."

"Yes what?"

"Yes, that's who I mean," Gavin answered, barely holding on to his temper.

He didn't have time for this. Every minute he wasted was a minute of normal that his son Sean wouldn't have.

"Why?"

"Why what?" Gavin asked.

"Why do you want her?"

In two seconds he'd grab this skinny, disrespectful spiky-haired worm and shake him till his piercings fell out. Huffing out a long breath, Gavin counted to ten. Manhandling a kid was most likely not the way to get what he wanted.

"It's none of your concern why I want her. I just do. Where is she?"

Spike shrugged. "Took Evil E to the office."

Evil E? Gavin really was in hell and it was getting more difficult by the second to believe M. J. Taylor was the angel he'd been promised by his son's doctor.

At that moment the door opened and a woman walked in accompanied by a male student. To Gavin's immense relief her blond hair was perfectly normal, worn straight to just past her shoulders. Her only piercings were silver hoops in her ears where piercings were supposed to be. She looked very young, but her navy slacks, long-sleeved white cotton blouse and sensible low-heeled shoes told him she wasn't a teenager. He couldn't say the same for the white-faced ghoul dressed in black beside her.

Gavin stared at the newcomer. "This must be the infamous Evil E."

The kid glowered more, if possible. "Famous? Is that good?"

"Infamous," she corrected, frowning at Gavin. "His name is Eveleth, you fill in the blanks." Then she looked at the kid. "Your homework is to look that word up in the dictionary."

"But I'm suspended." The tone was just this side of insolence.

"That doesn't mean you don't have homework. It simply means you have several days of time out to think about your behavior and figure out how to make it acceptable in the classroom before coming back to school."

"I didn't start it. He did." Lifting a finger, he pointed at Spike.

"You were supposed to be gone, Sullivan," she said to hardware face.

"I was waiting for him to come back for his stuff." The languid teen instantly jumped up and went for the ghoul, shoving the sub out of the way.

Recovering quickly, she got between them and tried to break it up. "Knock it off, you two," she grunted, pushing against ghoul's chest.

For all the attention they paid her, she might have been an ant between two chihuahuas. But the stubborn look on her face said she wasn't giving up. And that's when she got popped by a stray fist.

Gavin grabbed ghoul by the neck of his black T-shirt

and easily yanked him back. The physical intervention startled him long enough for Gavin to step between the two and sweep her out of the way with his arm.

"Back off before you get hurt," he ordered.

"They're my responsibility."

"The responsible thing to do would be to get help while I keep them from killing each other."

She nodded then picked up the phone on the wall and spoke to someone on the other end. Two minutes later the door opened and a beefy man who looked like campus security burst into the room and the teens froze. He took one look at the situation and shook his head.

"Office," he barked at the two combatants. "Now."

The two creeps glared at each other, breathing hard. Then Spike shot Gavin a drop-dead-bastard look before he sauntered out the door, every step broadcasting his message: screw you and every other adult on the planet. The ghoul followed in his cocky wake.

"You okay?" the guard asked the teacher.

"Fine," she said, letting out a breath.

Then the door closed and they were alone.

She met Gavin's gaze and her hand shook as she tucked a strand of silky blond hair behind her ear. "Thanks for your help."

"I'm glad I was here."

He studied her from head to toe, which didn't take long as she barely reached his shoulder. Her hair was fine and straight, a center part sending the silken strands to frame her small face. Her too long bangs caught in the thick, dark lashes framing her big blue eyes—eyes that tilted up, catlike at the corners, which was the only striking thing about her. She was slender, delicate and almost fragile-looking.

He wasn't sure what he'd expected, but when a woman was a man's first, best hope, he wanted someone more…more something. Wings, a halo and the ability to walk on water would be a definite plus. He'd figured taller, too. Then he noticed the red mark just forming below her eye and anger surged through him all over again.

He cupped her cheek in his palm and gently probed the area beginning to swell. "This needs ice. Are you really all right?"

Her beautiful eyes widened as she quickly backed away. "I'm fine," she said. "And grateful that you were here." Then she stared at him. "Why are you here?"

"I'm looking for M. J. Taylor."

"You found her. And you are?"

"Gavin Spencer."

She looked puzzled. "The name doesn't ring a bell. Do you have a student in one of my classes?"

He wanted to ask if he looked old enough to have a child in high school but decided he didn't want her to confirm it. What he'd been through with Sean had most certainly aged him. Instead he let his gaze wander over water stains in the acoustical ceiling and numerous desktop carvings in the thirty or so desks lined up in rows. This classroom was pretty grim.

"The real question is, why are you here? From what I just saw, tax money would be better spent on pepper spray and self-defense lessons than books and computers."

She laughed and it was a lovely sound. The shadows disappeared from the depths of her blue eyes.

"It's really not that bad. I like working with teenagers. They're funny and spontaneous. Today was just one of those days. An argument over a girl. Something happened at lunch." One slender shoulder rose in a shrug. "Teenage passion mixed with an abundance of hormones is not a pretty sight. Most of the time those two are actually quite pleasant and bright," she said, glancing at the door where the teenagers had disappeared.

"You sub for them a lot?"

"I'm a permanent substitute. I know. It's an oxymoron. I'm taking over the class for a teacher who recently had a baby."

Suddenly the sparkle was gone and the shadows returned, and he wondered why.

"What frightens me the most is that those two will be making the decisions about our welfare when we're in our declining years," he said.

"One hopes not those two in particular," she said, the corners of her lips curving up.

"You should do that more often."

"What?"

"Laugh. Smile."

Again the amusement disappeared and she was all

seriousness. And sadness. "Training the next generation—our caretakers—is no laughing matter."

"So why do you do it?"

"I have to make a living."

Everyone did. But he'd learned the hard way that if you had a lot of it, you became a target for the unscrupulous and morally challenged who wanted it. "You don't have to make a living like this," he said, glancing around again.

"That's presumptuous." Her gaze narrowed warily as she studied him. "You never answered my question. Are you here about a student?"

"I'm here because you're a speech pathologist."

"How did you know that?" she asked sharply.

"Dr. McKnight gave me your name." Gavin saw recognition in her expression, which told him she knew the neurologist.

"I *was* a speech therapist. Now I'm a teacher."

"A substitute," he pointed out. "Why?"

"I got burned out. This is less intense."

"Correct me if I'm wrong, but that fight was pretty intense." He looked around her classroom, then met her gaze. "Playing referee is better than helping children?"

"I believe I'm still helping children. But none of that is any of your business. So, Mr. Spencer, unless you have a student in my class that you want to discuss, I think we're finished—"

"I want to discuss a student. But he's not in your class. He's my son and he's in Kristin Hunter's first-grade class."

"I know her reputation. He's in good hands and couldn't be in a better school."

Gavin knew that. It's one of the reasons he'd bought his central California estate, Cliff House. He didn't want his son in private school as he'd been. And all his research about the area had confirmed that Northbridge Elementary was the best. There were things he couldn't give Sean—like a mother—because he'd taken steps to make sure the scheming opportunist who'd borne him a son would be out of their lives forever. But Gavin had grown up without benefit of maternal influence and he'd turned out okay. Sean would, too. There was no doubt in his mind. Because his boy had been doing great, until that terrible day—

"It is a good school," he agreed, pushing away the painful image.

"He's a lucky little boy."

Not so much, Gavin thought. If luck were involved, Sean would have been undamaged by the accident. But he *was* damaged and he needed therapy. Gavin intended to see that he got it.

"My son suffered a fall that resulted in traumatic brain injury. It changed him. He needs therapy, Miss Taylor, and you come highly recommended. From all accounts, you're the best."

"I'm sorry, Mr. Spencer—"

"Gavin."

"I don't do that anymore. I can't help your son." She turned away and walked over to the desk. After opening the bottom drawer, she pulled out her purse and slung the strap over her shoulder.

Before she could walk out the door, he curled his fingers around her upper arm to stop her. "Wait. You've made up your mind? Just like that?"

Surprised, she looked up at him, then at his hand, and he removed it. "Not just like that. There's no decision to make. I'm retired from the profession. Goodbye."

"I don't get it."

"School is over for today. I'm leaving now. It's customary to say goodbye."

"That's not what I meant and you know it. I'm told you have a gift for connecting with children. But you're turning your back. And you won't explain why?"

"I don't owe you an explanation." But there was sympathy in her expression when she added, "I'm sorry about your son. I truly hope you find someone for his therapy and that he makes a full recovery."

"I've already found someone," he pointed out.

"Not the right someone. I can't help him."

"That's not what I heard."

"Then you heard wrong."

M.J. had been fine, making real progress putting her life back together. Until Gavin Spencer. Two days ago she'd seen the sorrow and anguish in his eyes when he talked about his son. Sorrow and anguish. She knew them well, along with gut-wrenching grief. At least Gavin Spencer's son was still on this earth.

Pain tightened in her chest when she thought about her own son. Her Brian. Her sweet boy. She missed him terribly.

Still.

Always.

And, God help her, she couldn't put her heart and soul into another child. She just couldn't.

Tears filled her eyes and she blinked them away.

These troubling thoughts were all Gavin Spencer's fault. If he hadn't come to school the other day, all this would be buried as deep inside her as she could get it. But he'd brought it to the surface again.

She was tired when she guided her small, clunky compact car into the long drive leading to the house. As always, it came into view after she passed the tall cypress trees lining the road. She loved the big old Victorian where she'd grown up. More importantly, her mother and aunt loved the house that had been in the family for three generations.

And M.J. didn't want to be the generation that lost it. Since it was her fault ownership was in jeopardy, it was her responsibility to make sure it stayed in the family.

Frowning, she pulled up behind the sleek, shiny black Lexus sedan parked in the circular drive. When she shut off her ignition, the little car shuddered for several moments before going still. To the best of her knowledge, her mother and her aunt didn't know anyone who drove an expensive car like this. Their bingo, bunco and bridge-playing buddies zipped around in small compact cars—in better condition than hers.

As M.J. crossed the wide porch that wrapped around the house, she glanced once more at the black car and wondered if the sleazy bank official twirling the ends of his oily black mustache might be waiting inside to take her house away—in the very finest tradition of the *Perils of Pauline*. But that was silly and paranoid. She was making the payments on the mortgage her mother knew nothing about.

Inside, she proceeded to the kitchen, picking up the sound of voices. As she got closer, she realized one of them was masculine and disturbingly familiar. She stopped in the doorway and saw her mother sitting at the oak table with Gavin Spencer. Apparently he was a man who couldn't take no for an answer.

There was always a first time, M.J. thought, walking into the room. Two pairs of eyes—one blue, one very dark brown—stared at her.

"M.J., you're home. Finally. I was starting to worry." Evelyn Taylor fiddled with the china floral-patterned teacup in front of her. "After that incident at school the other day— Well, I worry that you're not going to come home at all."

"I'm fine, Mom."

Evelyn glanced at the man across from her. "M.J., you remember Gavin Spencer. He tells me he helped you break up the fight in your classroom."

"How's your cheek?" Gavin met her gaze.

She resisted the urge to touch the bruise that was

in a colorful state of healing—and none of the colors were especially flattering to her skin tone. "It's fine. And, yes, I remember him."

It would take a case of amnesia to forget Gavin Spencer. The man was tall and tanned and sinfully handsome. His almost black eyes snapped with intensity and his powerful, muscular body seemed to hum with tension and harnessed energy. His ride-to-the-rescue manner had unnerved her, along with his gentle touch. The heat of his fingers had seared a path clear through her.

Off balance, she'd answered his questions when normally she'd have clammed up. Clearly he had the power to get to her and she didn't like it. No man would get to her again—and she especially didn't trust one as glib and charming as Gavin Spencer. Charm and wit hid a multitude of sins. She was still paying the mortgage on that lesson, too.

"That school—" Her mother shuddered visibly. "It has the worst reputation in the district. I worry the whole time she's subbing."

"Mom—"

"I don't know why she insisted on taking an assignment there."

"Mom, don't start."

"It's no wonder they can't find subs for that campus."

"It's not that bad," she protested. But when she met Gavin's gaze, there was something predatory in his dark eyes, something warning that he'd use the information against her if he got the chance.

"Not that bad?" Evelyn heaved a huge sigh as she shook her blond head. "So you like getting between teenage boys with more testosterone than brains?"

M.J. glared at Gavin. Unable to hide it from her mother, she'd glossed over the cause of the cheek bruise. But he'd obviously filled in the blanks and she really wished he hadn't. "At school kids would call you a narc."

"Nice."

"Not so much. You ratted me out to my mother."

"Don't be mad at him," Evelyn protested. "We were simply chatting and he assumed I knew the particulars."

M.J. realized something bothered her more than the fact that he'd given her mother the ugly details. It was that he was here at all. How did he know where she lived? Why did he think her answer to his offer would be any different this time? She had no illusions that he was here for any other reason. She was an unremarkable woman, not the sort who inspired to-the-ends-of-the-earth passion in a man like him. He wouldn't notice her unless he wanted something only she could give. That was annoying enough, but even worse was that on some level it mattered to her.

But that was her problem and she would deal with it as she always did. On her own. All the same, she couldn't help being the tiniest bit grateful to have her mother here. When he asked again and she told him no again, she wouldn't be alone with him.

The thought had barely formed when Evelyn looked at the clock on the wall above the table and jumped up. "Good heavens, look at the time. I'm going to be late for the movie."

"Wait, Mom—"

"I can't. Mr. Spencer arrived just as Aunt Lil and I were on our way out the door. I sent her on ahead and told her to buy the tickets. You know how she hates to not be settled when the lights go down."

"But, Mom, I—"

Evelyn kissed her cheek. "See you later, sweetie. Nice to meet you, Mr. Spencer."

Before M.J. could say "boo," she was facing him alone. And she didn't particularly like it. He was too big, too good-looking, too dark and too persuasive. Too everything. And that made M.J. too nervous.

"What are you doing here?" she asked.

"I'd like to finish our conversation from the other day."

"As far as I'm concerned, it's finished."

"I'd like the opportunity to change your mind."

"You're wasting your time."

"It's my time."

"You can't change my mind," she warned.

"I don't believe that, Ms. Taylor."

M.J. had the uncomfortable feeling that the sheer force of his personality could make people do things against their will. But not in her case. After Brian died, she'd really tried to continue her work in speech therapy. But it simply hurt her heart too much to be around younger children. That made her hold back, avoid connecting. Protecting herself kept her from doing the job the way it should be done. She was no good to the kids now.

M.J. decided to change the subject. "How did you know where I live?"

"I didn't follow you."

"That's not what I asked."

He lifted one broad shoulder in a casual shrug. "This is the electronic age. With computer technology you can find anyone with very little information."

That was true. In this age of technology, it was pretty hard to hide. Not that she was. But still... "This feels very much like an invasion of my privacy. But you don't strike me as the sort of man who worries very much about breaking rules."

"A father has to do what a father has to do," he said, arrogant enough not to deny it.

In spite of his arrogance, she had a glimmer of respect for his parental determination, but then her own protective shields went back up. "And what is it you think you're doing?"

"Whatever I have to do to help my son. He's six years old."

Her chest tightened, as if a hand had reached inside and squeezed her heart. The crushing pain made it a struggle to catch her breath. Her son would have been six now.

She sucked in air. "I already told you, I don't work with children."

"The other day you said teens are children, too."

This was a bad time to learn she'd been right about

him collecting information to store up and use against her.

"High school doesn't count," she said defensively. Then she watched his dark eyebrows go up questioningly. She huffed out a breath. "Okay, technically they're children until eighteen. But high school kids are more like adults with impulse control issues."

"Look, let's stop splitting hairs. You need the work."

"Doesn't everyone?" she countered.

He stood and his eyes narrowed as he looked down at her. "Here's what I know. You have a reputation as a gifted children's speech pathologist. Sean's teacher and his doctor tell me you're a miracle worker and have a proven track record in getting results from children like my son. But you turned your back on a career—"

"You don't have any idea—"

"I don't have to." He held up a hand. "I'm a father. I'd slay dragons and storm fortresses if it would return my son to the way he was before the accident. I can't help him, but you can."

"Not anymore."

"I don't buy that. You got positive results in the past. Why not now?"

"I don't owe you an explanation."

"No. That's true. But the fact is I'm not giving up until I get one."

M.J. recognized the determination on his dark features. How dare he back her into a corner? Why wouldn't he just take no for an answer? Anger blazed through her. She was furious that he was putting her through this. She wanted him out of her house. And he might even leave. This time. But he'd be back. He had determination written all over him or he wouldn't be here now. Somehow M.J. was aware that he wouldn't leave her alone until he knew the reason she could no longer handle the job she'd once loved.

"An explanation?" She took a deep breath. "It's called survival, Mr. Spencer. I simply can't get wrapped up in a child. And that's what it takes to reach them. It's about dedication and focus. I can't do it anymore."

"Why?"

"I don't have the heart. My son took it with him when he died."

Chapter Two

Gavin had no idea what he'd expected her to say, but that wasn't it. Now *he* didn't know what to say. Looking at the suffering in her eyes was like staring into a bottomless pool of pain.

If the antique oak table wasn't between them, he was afraid he'd have taken her in his arms. "Look, M.J., I know how you feel—"

"No, Gavin." Her voice was brittle, as if she could shatter at any moment. She gripped the curved back of the oak chair in front of her until her knuckles turned white. "You couldn't possibly understand how I feel because you still have your son."

She was right. Sean's accident had opened a very

small window into what it would have been like to lose him, but fortunately it slammed shut and he still had his boy. Any comfort he could offer seemed pathetically inadequate, however sincere.

So he didn't offer any. "What happened to him?"

"Brian," she said. "His name was Brian."

"Brian." He nodded. "Tell me about him."

A small smile touched her lips. "He was a sweet boy. Quiet. Sensitive. Smart."

"Was he ill?"

Something in her expression said that would almost have been easier. "He was hit by a car. He ran out into the street after his ball. The driver couldn't stop in time."

Gavin nodded as the thought hovered in his mind. *Who was watching him?* But he couldn't ask. It was an accident. And he'd bet ever since it happened she'd been asking herself enough questions when she wasn't torturing herself with "if onlys."

That was something he *could* understand. If only Sean hadn't fallen on the rocks. If only he hadn't hit his head. If only… Sean could be his normal, active self.

But he couldn't. That's why Gavin was here. "It must be a comfort to have your mother. And Brian's father—"

For an instant her mouth tightened and something hot and harsh flashed through her eyes. "My husband died less than six months later. He wasn't ill, either," she said. "Car accident."

"I'm sorry." The words came out before he could stop them.

Fate really had her in its crosshairs and her expression said sorry didn't begin to help. It also made him think that there was much more she wasn't saying. Any or all of which was none of his business. Not that he didn't care. He wasn't a heartless bastard. But he wasn't here to rub her nose in the pain or to make her feel bad about the devastating losses she'd endured. His purpose was to secure the help his son needed to get his life back.

"Look, M.J., you're right. I have no idea how you feel. I can't begin to understand. And, to be brutally frank, I don't want to know. I came dangerously close to losing my son and that was enough."

"I'm sure that was difficult." Her grip on the chair eased.

"The time he spent in a coma was hell. Not knowing if he would live or die was torture."

"I can imagine."

And he knew she could. He could imagine that she wished to be in his shoes right now—to have the chance with her own child to bring him back from an injury. Maybe empathy would help him get through to her.

"Sean needs your help," he said simply.

"My answer is still the same. I'm sorry."

He was right about the words being pathetically inadequate. "I'm sorry" was the polite thing for her to say, yet it made him irrationally angry. Frustration gathered inside him and threatened to blow the lid off his temper as he tried to figure out what it would take to get through to her.

He glanced around the kitchen as if he'd find the answer there. The white appliances were spotlessly clean, but not very new. Old in fact. Wooden oak cupboards showed bare wood yellowed with age and in urgent need of refinishing. Faded yellow paint covered the walls and in the nook where the table sat, he could see chipping.

When he'd driven up to the front door, the Victorian had charmed him with its wraparound porch and turret. Then he'd looked closer and noticed shingles missing from the peaked roof and a loose section of railing that could use repair as well as a new coat of white paint.

Gavin looked at M.J. Her hair was pulled up, away from her face and fastened with a large clip, revealing a long graceful neck and good cheekbones. Again she was wearing slacks—black this time, with a long-sleeved cotton blouse, inexpensive and serviceable.

He raked his fingers through his hair. "Look, if it's about money…"

The term "got her back up" entered his mind. Her reaction was nearly imperceptible, but he'd swear her spine turned to steel. Or maybe he was just watching carefully because money had made him a target more than once. But the word "money" had definitely put a defensive look in her eyes, just for a moment, and her chin inched a bit higher. But she didn't respond.

"I can pay you well." He heard the guarded note in his own voice. He'd paid off a woman once. She'd deliberately gotten pregnant. Oh, he'd been a willing participant, but she'd lied about taking the pill. She'd threatened to terminate the pregnancy unless he paid her. He had because the life she carried was part of him. How such a mercenary, devious witch had produced a sweet-natured innocent like Sean he would never understand. But he'd fallen in love with his son at first sight and would do anything, pay anything, to bring him back. "Name your price."

"It's not about money, Gavin."

"In what fantasyland? It's always about money. Anyone could see I'm desperate. Why wouldn't you manipulate the situation to get more out of me?"

"You couldn't be more wrong."

"Everyone has a price," he snapped.

"That's quite a cynical attitude you've got there." She folded her arms over her chest as she observed him with her cool blue eyes.

"I earned it. School of hard knocks. You should know all about that," he said, looking at her shiner.

"I'm going to make an educated guess." Absently she touched her fingers to her cheekbone. "Your wife took you for a bundle. Frankly, instead of trying to tempt me with more money, you'd be better off channeling those bucks into better legal counsel. Next time get a prenuptial agreement."

"There were no nuptials so an agreement was never an issue. But I don't intend to let my guard down again."

"That's the first thing you've said that I can relate to."

He had no interest in relating to her and didn't give a damn whether or not she would trust again. That hinted at problems with her husband and the man was gone. The two of them wouldn't get a chance to work out their issues. Gavin wasn't unsympathetic. He simply didn't have time to waste. All he wanted was to hire her for his son's therapy.

He let out a long breath and willed himself to patience. "It doesn't take a mental giant to see that you need the money. I have lots of it. I can pay you extremely well for your expertise." God, it sounded like he was begging, but if that would change her mind, he'd do it. "Just say the word, M.J."

"I can't."

Two words, yet it sounded as if her heart was being ripped out. She'd told him that Brian had taken her heart, but Gavin didn't understand why that kept her from doing the job that, by all accounts, she was extremely good at.

"Why can't you? I would think your loss would motivate you, that you'd want to help injured children."

"You arrogant, pigheaded idiot. How dare you?" Anger flashed in her eyes and it was better than the sorrow. "What gives you the right to judge me?"

"I'm not judging—"

"The hell you aren't." She glared at him. "Not that it's any of your business, but it's too painful to be around young children."

"So it's self-protection?"

"Partly. But there's a clinical basis for my decision."

"I don't understand."

"It's simple really. I hold back emotionally. It's a response to pain, like pulling your hand away from fire. I can't connect with kids anymore—" She swallowed hard. "Whatever made me a good SLP is broken."

SLP. Speech language pathologist. Gavin had done his homework on the subject. And Sean's doctor had said she was the best. He needed her.

Correction: Sean needed her.

Gavin had seen her in action with teenagers. She'd found something positive to say about the two anti-social rebels. Whatever made her good with kids might be damaged, but he'd bet it wasn't broken.

But he noticed she was even more pale than that day in her classroom and more shaken up than she'd been after going a couple rounds with Evil E and hardware face. Her mouth trembled and her eyes were haunted, the bruise on her cheek standing out starkly against the fair skin. He'd stirred the pot of her feelings and should regret it, but guilt was a luxury he couldn't afford. Still, desperate as he was, it was clear that he'd pushed hard enough.

For now.

"I'd like to see for myself whether or not you've lost your edge." He slid his wallet from his back pocket and saw her gaze narrow as she frowned. After pulling out a business card, he dropped it on the oak table.

"Do me a favor. Just think about it." He walked past her and started toward the doorway.

"Do you ever say please, Gavin?"

"If it would change your mind I'd say it in a second."

"It wouldn't," she said. "I just wondered. Goodbye."

For now, he thought again.

M.J. set her steaming mug of green tea on the kitchen table, then sat down, unable to suppress a tired sigh. "It's good to be home."

Her mother set out three floral placemats followed by plates, napkins and utensils. While Evelyn set the table, Aunt Lil stirred something on the stove.

"Rough day?" her mother asked.

"Yes." M.J. saw the frown and regretted her honesty.

"You look tired, sweetie." Evelyn's mouth tightened with disapproval.

"I am." And not all of it was about the energy drain of educating teenagers. Some of it had to do with not sleeping well, and that was Gavin Spencer's fault.

How dare he dredge up all the painful memories? She'd worked hard the past two years, not to forget because that wouldn't happen, but to make herself remember the good things. To keep Brian alive in her heart. But it wasn't just about her memories. The dashing Mr. Spencer was disturbing, his intensity unsettling. He was alternately challenging and charming. But she refused to be charmed.

Her mother set a trivet in front of her on the table.

"M.J., I don't know why you refuse to take a less stressful, permanent position. It's not like the school district has an abundance of teachers."

"There's a need for educators on every level," M.J. admitted.

She remained on the substitute list because the per diem scale actually netted her more money. The downside was a different classroom every day. Except she was a permanent sub until the teacher she'd replaced returned from maternity leave.

"But sometimes I think the kids would learn just as well from a Sumo wrestler." She remembered Gavin saying she needed pepper spray and self-defense lessons. Today she agreed with him.

"What did the little stinkers do this time?" her mother asked.

"The usual. Not turning off cell phones. Someone with a camera phone trying to take a picture underneath an unsuspecting girl's skirt."

"Today's technological equivalent of sticking pigtails in the inkwell?" her mother asked wryly.

M.J. grinned. "Sort of. But what pushed me over the edge was the boy who jumped on his desk and let out a Tarzan yell during a test."

"It's too bad they won't let you smack knuckles with a ruler anymore. There's something to be said for corporal punishment and the old days." Evelyn nodded sagely.

"Now we send them to the dean of discipline," M.J. explained, feeling inadequate for not being able to deal with the situation. "But it's not fair to the other students when a teacher can't teach because one bozo disrupts the entire class."

Evelyn frowned. "I suppose. But I can't help wondering if you took a job in a different school things might be better."

M.J. was grateful when she was spared the need to lie because Aunt Lil walked over with a big container of split pea soup. She was older than her sister, a shorter version with blond hair and hazel eyes. Both were technically spinsters since neither of them had ever married. But unlike Evelyn, Lillian had never had children. She'd been like a second mother to M.J., a more diplomatic, less judgmental version.

"It's soup weather. March comes in like a lion, out like a lamb," Aunt Lil said. After setting down the large tureen, she automatically rubbed her wrist.

"Is your arm bothering you, Aunt Lil?"

The older woman smiled, a spunky look in her eyes as she held up her arm. "I could predict a cold front with these bones."

"I'm sure it's arthritis," her mother said.

"You should have let me know you wanted the soup on the table," M.J. said. "I'd have carried it over for you."

Guilt squeezed M.J. because she was responsible for the injury that had resulted in the arthritis. Years ago her aunt had tripped over something M.J. hadn't put away as ordered, and fell, breaking her wrist.

M.J. had never seen her mother so angry and still remembered the lecture.

Good girls always clean up their messes.

M.J. was doing just that as a substitute teacher. It was the best solution to her current financial mess because she simply couldn't go back to her career. And she was getting tired of explaining herself. A little over a week ago, she'd had a similar conversation with Gavin Spencer regarding her substitute teacher status. He'd been curious about why she refused a permanent assignment, too.

"There are advantages to a permanent teaching position, sweetie," her mother said, without missing a beat in picking up the thread of the conversation. "I should think knowing the good, bad and ugly about your students would take the edge off some of the stress."

"I'm fine, Mom. There is no edge."

Gavin had stood right here in this kitchen and said he'd like to see for himself whether or not she'd lost her edge as an SLP. She couldn't help admiring his determination to move heaven and earth to help his son. And she'd half expected him to show up again either here or at the high school. At the very least she'd figured he would phone her to renew his demand. But she hadn't heard a word.

The disappointment trickling through her was a surprise and made her feel particularly stupid. She should be relieved. Especially because memories of the intensity in his dark eyes gave her an odd, tight feeling around her heart. He was charismatic and persistent, a combination that would get him what he wanted with most people—women especially. But not with her.

However badly she needed the money, she simply couldn't do what he wanted. Her life was a leaky rowboat and she was bailing as fast as she could. So far, she was staying afloat. Barring another disaster, she could meet her financial obligations and no one would be the wiser. She'd rather walk barefoot on broken glass than have her mother and aunt find out the only home they'd ever known was always one paycheck away from being snatched out from under them.

Her mother rested her hands on the table and leaned forward. "M.J., I just don't understand why you're making things harder—"

"Dinner's ready," Aunt Lil interrupted.

M.J. shot the older woman a grateful look. "This smells wonderful, Aunt Lil. I love your soup."

"Your aunt is a good cook," Evelyn agreed. She sat across from M.J. "I never had time to nurture my inner chef."

M.J. felt another twinge. Her mother was a single mom before the needs of single moms were commonly recognized. It wasn't M.J.'s fault, but she felt guilty that her mother had worked so hard to provide for her. The only thing Evelyn hadn't worried about was the roof over their heads because the house had been in the family for so long. M.J. intended to see that didn't change.

"It takes more than time to be a cook, Ev," her aunt said gently. She sipped from her spoon and nodded with satisfaction. "Yagottawanna."

M.J. laughed. "Excuse me?"

"You have to want to do it. You're a teacher, dear. You should understand. Some people go through the motions because they have to. Others just have the desire to be successful. Any fool who can read can follow a recipe. But a good cook has a calling, a need to experiment, a love of working with food."

"I suppose I didn't get that gene," her mother admitted.

"Me, either," M.J. said. She looked down at her empty bowl and realized she'd scarfed down the contents. "But I'd appreciate it if you'd write down everything you put in this soup so this fool could have a recipe to read."

"I'll do that as best I can. And thank you, dear. I'm glad you like it."

After dinner, the sisters cleaned up and M.J. was shooed out of the kitchen to rest. Since she had papers to grade, that wasn't going to happen. She grabbed the backpack with her work and started up the stairs to her room when she noticed the mail on the sofa table in the entryway.

Scooping it up, she headed upstairs. Her room was just above the kitchen and had the same bay window, with a chair and ottoman filling it. On one wall sat her queen-size bed, the pink chenille spread neatly covering it. Her desk sat just inside the door and she set the mail down there.

The top envelope caught her eye when she noticed the official-looking return address from a mortgage company. She'd learned to loathe official-looking letters. It was never good news. Her stomach knotted and her hands shook as she opened the envelope.

M.J. read through it several times, hoping she was getting it wrong, then realizing she wasn't that lucky. The words *second mortgage, balloon payment, six months* and enough zeroes to make her eyes cross just put a gaping hole in her leaky little rowboat. This was the disaster she'd been afraid would sink her and it was a beaut.

After Evelyn's mild heart attack three years ago, her mother and aunt had put the title in M.J.'s name because they weren't getting any younger. M.J. hadn't known about her husband's compulsive gambling. Only after his death had she learned that he would do anything, use anyone, to get the money to fund his obsession. Some methods were more underhanded than others. She wasn't sure how he'd managed the first mortgage let alone this one. The bill was due and payable in six months, she didn't have the money, and she *was* liable. In addition to borrowing against the house, he'd maxed out numerous credit cards, some of them in her name, all of which she was responsible for. Thanks to him, her credit was ruined and she couldn't borrow a dime.

M.J. dropped into her desk chair before her trembling legs gave out. What was she going to do?

She wasn't sure how long she sat staring at the letter before dropping it on the desk blotter. Tucked into a pocket was the card Gavin had given her. She picked it up and stared at the no-nonsense black block letters. Gavin Spencer, CEO, Spencer Technology, Inc.

"I hate that you were right, Gavin. But everyone does have a price."

M.J. picked up the phone and dialed the number on the card.

Chapter Three

M.J. breathed a sigh of relief when her little old car coughed and wheezed, then shuddered off in front of Gavin's house. When giving directions, he'd said Cliff House overlooked the Pacific Ocean on a bluff, but with everything else on her mind, it hadn't quite registered that getting there involved a serious incline.

"The little car that could. Barely." She patted the dashboard approvingly, then got out.

She'd agreed to meet Gavin here at five o'clock and it was getting dark. Late-afternoon clouds had rolled in off the ocean and the large gray house blended in, except for the intricate and elaborate white trim that outlined the roof, windows and second-floor deck. The expanse of lawn was neatly trimmed as were the marguerites and privets bordering it. California cypress grew thick around the perimeter, giving the estate privacy.

She looked around again and knew she was putting off going inside. "Procrastination is a crime. It only leads to sorrow. I can stop it anytime, I think I will tomorrow." It was a rhyme she recited to her students, teasing them into taking action. It was time to take her own advice. "I hate that rhyme," she mumbled.

Taking a deep breath, she followed the walkway to the double-door entry. As the mist rolled in, she shivered, feeling like the plucky heroine of a Gothic romance novel. The difference was, she wasn't plucky. Desperation was her only motivation. If she had a choice, she'd get back in her little car and go as fast as she could back down the hill.

She rang the bell and, through the oval etched glass in the door, she could see lights inside and someone coming. Bracing herself, she prepared to see Gavin again. When a tall, trim, gray-haired man opened the door, she was surprised.

"Hi," she said. "I'm—"

"Ms. Taylor. I'm Henderson, the caretaker of Cliff House. Mr. Spencer said to expect you. He had planned to be here when you arrived, but was delayed at the office. He'll be here shortly and sends his apologies. I'll introduce you to Sean."

"Thank you." It was the polite response, but M.J.

wanted to tell him not to do her any favors. She dreaded this with every fiber of her being.

"My wife, Lenore, is the housekeeper. She's watching over the boy in the family room."

M.J. nodded as she glanced around. The entryway ceiling must be twenty feet high. Twin staircases curved up to the second floor. As she followed Henderson through the house, she had a fleeting impression of elegant furniture in serene shades of celery and hunter green. In the artwork and glassware there were splashes of red, gold and orange. Beige tile gave way to plush carpet as they moved through the house.

Just off the kitchen with black granite-covered island and countertops, they stopped in the family room. A large sea-foam green sectional filled one corner with a huge flat-screen TV across from it.

An older woman sat on the sofa. Beside her, a recliner built into the sectional was pushed back with the footrest extended. Beneath it, a boy lined up little plastic dinosaurs, then set two pterodactyls on the footrest above, poising them to swoop down on the tyrannosaurus rex and the triceratops. She knew the names because Brian had loved them and constantly begged her to read him dinosaur books.

Emotion tightened in her chest and spread into her throat.

Henderson walked farther into the room. "Lenore, Sean, this is Ms. Taylor."

A petite, brown-eyed brunette, Lenore smiled warmly. "Welcome to Cliff House."

The polite thing to say would be that it was nice to be here. But it wasn't nice. At this moment she'd give anything if she hadn't been raised to be polite. M.J. wanted to turn and run from toys that were scattered on the floor, little cars small enough for little hands. A small boy in blue jeans and long-sleeved, striped T-shirt. His white sneakers were scuffed because active boys were hard on shoes. It was all so familiar, and looking at it produced a physical ache.

"Ms. Taylor?" There was concern in Henderson's voice.

"Yes." She let out a long breath as she slid her hands into the pockets of her sweater and looked at them. "Lenore. Sean. Hi."

"Sorry I'm late." Gavin rushed into the room and Sean smiled, then instantly jumped up and raced to his father.

Brian used to do that when she got home from work. Tears burned her eyes and she held her breath, waiting for the squeal of delight when Gavin swung his son into his arms. But it never came.

Gavin took the boy's weight on his forearm and their faces were close together. There was no question of paternity. Sean was the image of his father. "Hi, buddy. Did you have a good day?"

Sean nodded.

"You met Ms. Taylor? M.J."

This time the boy pointed at her and nodded.

"Good. She's going to help you talk again."

Gavin bent to set him down and the boy clung for several moments.

When his father straightened, Sean looked up at him, dark eyes wide and questioning. He was a beautiful little boy and would grow into a handsome man, just like his father. She wondered if he'd also inherited Gavin's intensity, determination and charm. All of that would help him be successful in the weeks of therapy ahead.

Gavin ran his hand over the boy's dark hair. "Daddy needs to talk to M.J., son. You stay with Lenore." When Sean pointed to his dinosaurs, Gavin said, "That's right. Have fun with your toys."

The boy shook his head, then pointed to Gavin and his dinosaurs.

"I can't play right now, buddy. Later." He looked at her. "We can talk in my office."

She didn't miss the flash of disappointment on the child's face before Gavin put his hand at the small of her back and urged her from the room. She accompanied him down a hall and into an office that was as elegant as it was masculine. The walls were oak-paneled, with a matching desk dominating the center of the hunter-green carpet. One wall was entirely windows with French doors looking out on the ocean.

Two leather wing chairs were in front of the desk and he indicated she should sit.

Gavin took off his suit coat and draped it across the high back of the desk chair. He sat across from her, loosened his red tie and rolled up the long sleeves of his white dress shirt to just below the elbows. As if that wasn't masculine enough, she noticed that his jaw was dark with five o'clock shadow. It gave him a dangerous look that set off a fluttering sensation in her stomach. Again her survival instincts were telling her to run, but this time for a different reason.

"So," Gavin said, folding his hands on the desk. "Thanks for coming. Can I ask what changed your mind?"

She wanted to tell him he was free to ask, but she didn't have to answer. Except, given her firm, outspoken objection to his offer, it was a fair question. That didn't mean he was entitled to the whole truth. "Let's just call it a moment of weakness."

He studied her for several seconds, then shrugged. "It doesn't really matter. The point is you're here. And I'm grateful."

Don't be, she wanted to say. "Sean's injury was to the left side of his brain," she said, getting straight to the point. They had no reason to do small talk.

"Yes. How did you know?"

"That's where language function is controlled."

Gavin nodded and his expression was grim. "He used to be a chatterbox."

"With TBI, or traumatic brain injury," she added, although probably he'd heard the term more than he wanted, "the jolt to the head disrupts brain function and it isn't just language that's affected."

"The doctor told me."

"Did he also make you aware that reading, social

skills such as impulse control, gauging consequences for a behavior and acting out because of frustration can also be affected by the injury?"

He nodded. "Medically, Sean's come as far as he can."

"Do you have a prognosis?"

"The neurologist feels that with cognitive and physical therapy, Sean has a good chance to regain brain function lost due to the trauma."

"Good. I'll need to do a series of tests on Sean to see where he is, then work up a treatment plan."

"Okay."

She knew a therapist was the driving force in treatment. But, like a general, she needed to martial all the forces at her disposal. She needed to know who she could count on. "Gavin, clearly you're dedicated to Sean's care. What about Sean's mother? Will she—"

"She won't be involved," he snapped.

M.J. almost shivered at the ice-cold tone of his voice. "You should know that TBI kids typically progress faster when both parents become involved in the process."

"Sean's mother doesn't have any contact with him."

"I see."

"I doubt it." His gaze narrowed.

True. If she still had her son, nothing and no one could keep her from him.

"You're right," she agreed. "I don't see. But I can make a guess that she's the woman who worked you into that cynical attitude of yours and is responsible for you keeping your guard up."

"You'd be correct." A muscle jumped in his jaw. "All you need to know is that Sean is better off without her."

M.J. couldn't help being curious. He'd never married Sean's mother and he was raising the boy by himself. He believed money could buy everything and everyone. It didn't require ugly details to see that the woman had really done a number on him. Sympathy started to stir inside M.J. and she shut it down. He was a client, her employer. As one parent to another, she sympathized with what he was going through, but she didn't want to feel anything for him as a man.

"What about grandparents?" she asked.

Gavin shook his head. "My father passed away about two years ago."

M.J. waited for more, but he didn't say anything about extended family on his mother's side. When curiosity stirred again, she ignored it. "Who takes care of him when you're at work?"

"Henderson and Lenore. They've been with me since before Sean was born."

"So they're like family?"

"Yes. They're devoted to my son."

"Good." She met his gaze. "But you're the most important person in his world."

"And I'll do whatever it takes. You can count on me."

She nodded. "Does Sean speak at all?"

"Not much," he said ruefully. "A word here and

there, but not complete sentences." Worry etched lines in his handsome face. "He was perfect before the accident."

"He's a beautiful child," she said softly. Something stirred inside her and again she shut it down.

Gavin met her gaze, his own stark with a father's pain. "I want him back the way he was."

M.J. nodded her understanding. Any parent in his position would feel the same. Now wasn't the time to tell him Sean's accident had changed him forever. No one could go through what he had and be the same as he was. The question was how much brain function could be regained.

To accomplish the best case scenario, M.J. needed to establish a bond with the child. How was she going to do that when every instinct urged her to shut down? To disengage from him? Once, she would have hugged Sean when introduced. Touched him. Shaken his little hand. Now she wouldn't. She couldn't.

She hoped Gavin hadn't made a mistake hiring her and that she hadn't made a colossal error in judgment by accepting the job.

She stood and slipped her hands into the pockets of her sweater. "I'll do my best to help Sean."

That was also the truth. Although it wasn't much, she'd give everything she had left. But that didn't include her heart. Not for the child. Or his father.

It had been four weeks since M.J. had first come to Cliff House. Gavin had cut short a meeting at work so that he could be here before she left today. Standing in the shadows just outside the room, he could observe, but the two didn't notice him.

He was frustrated as he watched her on the family room floor playing with Sean. They were doing a dinosaur puzzle and hadn't noticed him yet. First she had the boy trace the space where the piece fit, then run his finger around the piece itself before fitting the irregular cardboard into the right place.

"Good job." She smiled at the boy.

What the heck did this have to do with helping Sean to speak again?

"Now," she said. "Brush your finger over the next space like I showed you. Do the same with the piece that goes there, then put it where it belongs."

Concentration furrowed Sean's forehead as he complied with the first directive. Then he blinked at M.J., confusion in his eyes.

"It's okay, sweetie. Trace the space." When he nodded, she smiled. "Good. Now what?"

The boy thought for a few moments, then put the puzzle piece in place.

"Way to go, kiddo. High five." She held up her hand and Sean slapped it.

The boy grinned at her before rolling around on the floor.

"I think we need to get rid of the wiggles," she said, standing.

She shook her hands using a wrist motion and Sean imitated. He copied when she stretched her neck then moved her head from side to side before bending to touch her toes. That gave Gavin a good view of her fanny, which was covered by the usual black pants. Since she'd been coming, he'd dropped by the therapy sessions a couple of times for a few minutes and this was the first he'd noticed that she had some pretty nice curves going on. Then she smiled at Sean and the expression transformed her.

She was prettier than Gavin realized. That didn't make him happy.

When he moved to the center of the doorway, Sean immediately saw him and grinned, then raced across the room, but there was no shouted greeting. Gavin's chest tightened. He longed to hear his son say, "Daddy."

Gavin brushed his hand over his son's hair as the boy caught his leg. When he looked at M.J., he saw that her smile had disappeared and found he missed it.

"Hey, buddy. How are you?" When the child pointed to the puzzle, then M.J., Gavin said, "I see. You've been playing with M.J."

"He likes puzzles," she said. "He's good at them."

"Of course he is. He's a Spencer." But being good at puzzles wasn't the progress Gavin expected. He met her gaze. "I'd like to speak to you. Do you have a couple minutes?"

"Of course."

After Sean was settled in the kitchen with Lenore, Gavin looked across his desk at M.J. She sat stiffly, her hands linked in her lap.

He was still remembering her smile and irritated because he did. "I'll get right to the point. As far as I can see, there's no change in my son's condition."

"I agree."

That surprised him. He was accustomed to spin and excuses when the desired result wasn't achieved. M.J. stared back at him without apology.

"I thought there would be noticeable progress. Can you explain why there isn't?"

"Yes." Her chin lifted slightly. "Because Sean is a little boy, not a business project. He'll go at his own speed, not the timetable you mandate."

"Based on your glowing references, I just thought—" He ran his fingers through his hair.

"You thought I could snap my fingers, wiggle my nose and he'd be cured?"

"Something like that," he admitted.

"This isn't about a cure. It's about regaining the function that was lost." Her tone was patient, soft, soothing. "It's going to take a lot of work. And that will take time."

Gavin had noticed the way she was with Sean today. She'd been playful, firm, determined and lively. There was a sweetness about her that seemed to come from within. It appeared genuine and unforced, a natural extension of herself—very real. And that smile. She was pretty when she smiled, and he wanted to think of her only as plain.

"How long?" He heard the edge to his voice and suspected it was fear. He was afraid his boy would never be okay. If only this were a disease and ten days of antibiotics the course of treatment. He wanted his son back now. At the very least, he wanted guarantees and a time frame.

"I don't know."

"You can't make a guess based on experience? When my father was dying of cancer, the doctors gave me an estimate and it turned out to be almost to the day," he snapped.

"That's an entirely different situation. Medical doctors have studies and data and tests that help them make an educated guess. In situations like this, there can't be a specific timetable. Every child is different. Every injury is different."

"Can you give me a ballpark estimate?"

"No." She met his gaze. "But I can tell you that it might go faster if you get involved in the therapy."

"You mean, doing puzzles?"

"That was brain exercise and therapy for hand-eye coordination," she said.

"It looked like playing to me."

"If therapy techniques weren't disguised as fun, how cooperative do you think Sean would be?"

"Obviously, I don't know anything about speech language therapy. How much help could I be?"

"I can show you what to do. I distinctly remember that you promised to do whatever it takes to help your son. I believe you said I could count on you." The tender tone was gone, replaced by toughness.

And she was right; he had promised. She met him

toe-to-toe and wouldn't blink. Part of him respected her for that. On the other hand, he didn't as a rule notice when an employee's smile made her pretty. That thought was followed by irrational anger, which didn't bode well for tact.

"You're the expert, Ms. Taylor. It's why I pay you the big bucks."

Any earlier traces of warmth and patience disappeared. "Is this third degree really about Sean?"

"What do you mean?" he asked.

"Are you implying that I'm dragging out a child's therapy for financial gain?"

"Are you?"

"That would be unethical." Her mouth tightened and anger flashed in her eyes, making them a darker shade of blue.

You're beautiful when you're angry. The thought jumped into his mind before he could stop it. In that moment, she was striking. Something inside him responded, stirred to life, and he regretted it instantly.

Again his temper took over. "This wouldn't be the first time someone held a child's life hostage."

"What does that mean?" she demanded.

It meant he'd been stupid once. A woman had used his child to get to him and he wouldn't let it happen a second time. M.J. seemed warm and real and sincere. But what if he was wrong again?

When he didn't answer, she stood. "Gavin, you've made it clear that you believe everyone has a price. But I'm not everyone and you don't know me."

He was getting to know her, and he wasn't sure yet if that was a problem. "What's your point?"

"Just this—you were the one who badgered me into taking this job. If you don't trust me, I'll gladly walk out that door. You're paying me for my skill, but you have no idea what it's costing me. That little boy is—"

The bleak expression was back in her eyes. "What, M.J.?"

She swallowed several times, then caught her top lip between her teeth. Finally she said, "Sean is the same age Brian would have been."

That took the heat out of his temper. "I didn't know."

"There's a lot you don't know about me. And I don't know you. I don't know why you're cynical and determined to mistrust everything I do. I did warn you that I'm not the way I was, that my abilities are impaired, but you insisted. I promised you that I would do the best I could under the circumstances. But if you've changed your mind, say the word and it would be my pleasure to resign."

Gavin studied her. He could almost see the anger drain out of her, replaced by weariness. Dark circles bruised the soft skin beneath her eyes and it had nothing to do with getting popped while breaking up a high school scuffle. But it might have a lot to do with the hard knocks in her life.

On top of that, she taught full-time and worked with Sean three evenings a week. He'd just seen for himself that the therapy demanded a high level of energy and attention. It wouldn't violate his rules to give her the benefit of the doubt.

"I haven't changed my mind," he said.

She met his gaze. "If you do, don't hesitate to let me know."

Then she walked out. After she said goodbye to Sean, Gavin followed her and opened the front door, but she walked out without looking back. She got in the car and turned the key in the ignition several times before the engine caught.

He watched the red taillights of her old car until they disappeared in the fog. He'd never thought he was the type to form an opinion about a person based on appearance, but now he wasn't so sure. He'd thought M. J. Taylor pale and plain, but a few minutes ago he'd seen flash and fire in her. There was more to her than he'd first thought and he suspected there was far more than the little she'd revealed.

He realized he was staring into the swirling mist and closed the door. If only he could close off his thoughts as easily. He hadn't spent this much mental energy on a woman in a long time.

And that time had been a disaster.

Chapter Four

M.J. put games, puzzles and flashcards in her backpack, then glanced around her room to see if there was anything else she might be able to use with Sean in today's session. It was interesting that the techniques came right back to her as if she hadn't been away for a year and a half. Somehow it seemed disloyal to her little boy's memory, but her punishment was the pain of seeing Gavin's little boy and being reminded that she would never see her own son again.

There was a soft knock on her door. "Come in," she called.

Her mother opened it, then frowned. "You're going out?"

"Yeah. Sean Spencer."

She'd explained to her mother why Gavin had stopped by that day. The cover story was that his urgency and determination had eventually worn down her resistance and he'd convinced her to work with his child. Evelyn seemed pleased that she was finally putting the past behind her and moving forward.

"You look tired, M.J."

That didn't even begin to describe how she felt. She was beyond tired and had settled into a permanent state of exhaustion. The extra strain of burying emotion and bracing herself to see Sean's achingly sweet young face took every ounce of energy she had left after teaching high school.

But admitting as much would mean explaining why she was working two jobs, and M.J. couldn't go there. "I'm all right, Mom."

"All right isn't fine. Why are you doing this after an exhausting day teaching those ungrateful teenage dweebs?"

M.J. smiled at her slang-challenged mother. "As weird as it sounds, I like them. And let's not forget, today's dweebs are tomorrow's grown-ups."

"Then you could give up the other job." Evelyn didn't smile. "You don't have to work with Sean. Gavin could find another therapist. Surely you don't need the money."

It was an old, tired conversation. After M.J.'s husband died, Evelyn had assumed he had life insurance. Nothing could be further from the truth. In fact, he'd left her with a mountain of debt she hadn't known about.

Yes, Gavin could hire another therapist. But M.J. desperately needed the extra money to clean up the mess of the mortgages and other bills that her mother was better off not knowing about. Unfortunately that meant no whining, and M.J. really wanted to whine.

Instead she put on a happy face and bypassed the issue of money entirely. "Sean is a bright boy. Full of energy."

"How's he doing?"

M.J. set her full backpack by the door then let out a sigh when she sat on the chair. The card Gavin had given her was still tucked into her desk blotter. She traced the bold, black letters of his name. His bold, handsome face flashed into her mind and she shivered.

She met her mother's gaze. "Sean's making steady progress."

Even if his father couldn't see it. Was Gavin too demanding? He wanted results, but what father wouldn't in the same situation? Any parent who didn't want their child to go back to the way they were before an accident was a parent who needed serious psychotherapy. And a mother who'd lost a child needed something she could never get back.

Evelyn patted her shoulder. "I'm glad he's doing better. But I'm still concerned about you. All day in the classroom and that doesn't include time spent doing lesson plans or grading papers. Then three nights a week you work with Sean. You're going to make yourself ill."

M.J. didn't want to think about what would happen if she couldn't work. So she didn't. "Don't worry about me, Mom. The schedule is intense and I'll admit it's draining sometimes, but I'll be fine."

As long as Gavin didn't decide his son wasn't progressing quickly enough and fire her. That was something else she didn't want to think about. If it happened, she had no idea what she'd do. For the sake of her sanity, she decided not to borrow trouble. Right now she had enough to worry about, thank you very much.

Evelyn studied her. "Are you sure you're all right?"

"I'm sure."

When Evelyn's expression filled with sympathy and sorrow, it was clear she was talking about the child they'd lost. "You're not just doing all of this to keep yourself too busy to think?"

Even if that were true, M.J. thought, she was a dismal failure because she was thinking all the time. Unfortunately some of those thoughts were about Gavin. What had happened to make him so cynical? Was that having a negative impact on Sean? Not only was Gavin aggressively taking up her conscious mind, his too handsome image drifted through her dreams. The dark intensity on his face. The glittering passion in his eyes was seared into her subconscious and she couldn't seem to forget how determined he was to have his son back. If desire were enough, that boy would be whole again.

Desire.

The single word made her tremble. How stupid was that? She barely knew Gavin; she hardly ever saw him. It seemed he made himself more scarce after she'd tried to get him involved in Sean's therapy. But facts were facts. Even if she was capable of caring, a man like him would never be interested in someone like her. How weird was she that the thought made her wistful? She should embrace facts without question.

M.J. said with absolute certainty, "I'm definitely not keeping myself too busy to think."

"Okay." Her mother nodded. "You're a big girl."

There were times she wished she wasn't, but never more than when Gavin looked at her with that mysterious expression in his dark eyes. She would give almost anything to know what he was thinking. Almost.

"Tell me about your millionaire."

That surprised her. "You mean, Gavin?"

"Do you have another one?" Evelyn asked.

"First of all, he's not mine."

"But he is a millionaire. I read the paper."

"Even the society pages?"

Her mother smiled. "I get bored waiting for the doctor and the hairdresser."

M.J. grinned back. "I'm shocked and appalled."

"Don't tell your aunt."

"Our little secret."

"So, what's he like?"

It was on the tip of her tongue to say he was a

hottie, but M.J. held back. He definitely was that. And so much more.

"You met him," M.J. said, not trusting herself to talk about the brooding intense man.

"I remember. He's not the kind of man a woman could forget. Not even an old one," she said with a grin.

M.J. understood all too well. "He's certainly a concerned father."

She admitted that concern, although she'd been infuriated by his insinuation that she was dragging out the therapy for personal gain. He'd told her he didn't trust anyone, but she was only beginning to realize how deeply ingrained the mind-set was. Whatever happened to him must have been bad for him to still be so wary. He'd admitted Sean's mother was the guilty party. And she knew the woman wasn't involved in her child's life. That was just wrong.

M.J. would give anything to have Brian here with her. The familiar pain took its place in her chest and she wondered how a mother could abandon her child.

How could a woman abandon Gavin?

The thought came out of nowhere and she shook her head, as if that would clear away the feeling. If she couldn't get rid of it, she'd be forced to admit she was attracted to the man. It was a complication she didn't need.

"What's his house like?"

"Big. Beautiful. Overlooking the ocean. It's a dream house. Like you'd expect a millionaire to have."

Evelyn thought about that. "I'll bet it doesn't have

the same character as this place and all the tradition of several generations."

"That's true." Her stomach knotted. "He has a mansion, but it's a house, not a home."

And Sean was being raised by staff, not family.

True, Gavin was a working father. He had financial resources. But all the money in the world didn't replace a mother's love. The question was why Sean's mother was out of the picture. Was it by choice or had Gavin "fired" her because she didn't meet his expectations?

He was a demanding man and that concerned her for Sean's sake.

She'd seen the way the boy looked at his father, as if the sun rose and set on him. She'd also seen Gavin rush in or not show up at all while she was there. He worked long hours and she could understand that. But was it by chance or by choice? Was he paying the staff to parent and her to put the boy back together?

Children wanted to please their parents. Even the antisocial teens she taught wanted approval whether they admitted it or not. M.J. couldn't help feeling that Sean would progress faster if his father got involved with the therapy. That would mean spending more time with Gavin, as if her life wasn't already complicated enough.

After six weeks, three sessions a week, M.J. wasn't having much luck in distancing her emotions from Sean Spencer. They were on the floor in the family room as she looked at his easy smile and dark eyes. She smiled back and a little more ice melted from around her heart. If she weren't so tired…

But this session was almost finished. Memory function was critical in his progress and M.J. had been working on that in subtle ways. The goal was to give him several commands all at once and have him perform the tasks without a reminder. The beauty was that Sean thought they were simply playing catch with the large red ball.

Her intention was to practice hand-eye coordination at the same time they worked on flexing his memory. "Catch it, Sean."

He held out his chubby little arms, but the foam ball hit him in the face because he didn't react fast enough. "Ball."

He giggled and rolled on the floor because to him it was just a game. He was saying more isolated words and the pleasure of that progress almost blocked out the prick of pain that she always felt when she watched his typical active-little-boy antics. Almost, but not quite.

"Good try, sweetie. Throw it back." When he did, the aim was way off and she bent to retrieve it. "Let's do it again. Catch the ball and throw it back."

She tossed the ball again and this time he caught it. He scrunched it between his hands and she waited to see if he'd remember. He drew his arm back and let fly.

"Good job, Sean." That was two. "Catch the ball and throw it back."

"Way to go," she praised when he did.

They repeated this process—Sean retrieved the ball when he missed, then threw it back. She knew a normal six-year-old had a fairly short attention span and waited for a sign that he was restless. It came when he bent over and let out an exaggerated sigh.

"Okay, that's enough playing catch."

He'd done very well. It was just about time for their session to end, but she wanted to try one more thing, just to see.

"Do you want to play another game?"

When he nodded enthusiastically, she laughed. "Okay. You worked so hard playing catch. Now we have to stretch. So, I want you to touch your toes, rub your tummy and clap your hands."

He nodded, then clapped his hands and waited.

"Touch your toes, rub your tummy and clap your hands."

He rubbed his tummy and touched his toes.

"One more time, Seanster. Touch your toes, rub your tummy, clap your hands."

He touched his toes, rubbed his tummy and clapped his hands.

M.J. blinked. "Good job."

She was excited, but tried not to react differently. "Want to do it again?"

He nodded, eager to play.

"Okay." She thought for a moment. "Rub your head, clap your hands, flap your arms."

He rubbed his head, clapped his hands and flapped his arms.

This was big—really big. Sequencing actions exercised brain muscles and the hope was that he would eventually string words together. M.J. only grinned, but inside she was pumping her arm and shrieking with excitement. She'd forgotten the adrenaline rush of breakthrough moments.

"Way to go, Seanster. High five." When he slapped her hand, she said, "Another one. You did an excellent job today."

"I take it something good happened?" Gavin stood in the doorway.

M.J.'s heart beat faster. "Your daddy's home, Sean."

The child raced by her and grabbed his father's leg. He looked up. "Daddy."

Gavin stared at the child as if he couldn't believe he'd heard right. "Hey, buddy," he said, a catch in his voice.

He bent to hug the boy and the sight of chubby little arms that wouldn't go all the way around that strong neck brought the sting of tears to M.J.'s eyes.

"I never thought I'd hear that from him again." Gavin's gaze was filled with shock and awe. "I can't believe it."

"Progress," she said, unable to filter all the sarcasm from her tone.

"Okay. I get it. I was a jerk." His self-deprecating tone was disarming.

"You'll get no argument from me."

He grinned, then stood and brushed his hand over his son's hair. "Sean, it's almost time for dinner."

The boy looked back at her and pointed. They'd been through this before. He wanted her to stay.

"I'm sorry, sweetie. I can't. It's time for me to go."

Not only because she was exhausted, but she still had schoolwork to do. And he needed to be alone with his father to celebrate this wonderful moment. But Sean walked over to her and held up his arms. She knew he wanted to hug her and every survival instinct she possessed cried out against it.

But when she looked into that sweet face, flushed with triumph, she couldn't stop herself. It was automatic. She bent and hugged him. Then the little boy raced back to his father, oblivious to the capital-M Moment.

Gavin was still wearing amazement on his face. "How did you do it?"

"I didn't do anything. Sean's been working very hard on the threes."

He frowned. "Want to translate?"

"Three commands to perform. Doing three things in a row is brain exercise."

"Like pumping iron for the mind."

She wanted to smile at the analogy, but held back. "That's exactly what I mean. The technique stimulates memory function. The goal is for him to remember and string words together."

"It looks like it's working. I thought I'd never hear him call me daddy again."

Before she knew what was happening, Gavin grabbed her in his arms and lifted her off her feet, spinning her in a circle. She hung on out of instinct because given a choice she wouldn't have touched him at all. She didn't want to be this close and now she knew why. He smelled way too good. His body was too solid, too warm, too masculine. She was breathless and not just from the spinning motion.

When he set her down, she backed up a step, then looked at the boy. "I know it feels slow, but he's making good progress."

"Of course he is." Gavin smiled, grabbed the giggling boy up, and swung him around as the child giggled with delight. "He's a Spencer," he added, setting the child down.

Sean tugged on his father's hand and M.J. saw the expectation in his eyes, knowing he wanted more attention. But when Gavin looked down, he only ruffled the boy's hair. "Go wash up for dinner, son."

Sean shook his head and pointed at her.

"She already said she can't stay, buddy."

Sean shook his head and frowned, his body language clearly indicating he didn't like that answer. Gavin saw it, too.

"It's time to clean up, Sean. Now."

The boy wasn't happy, but he dragged himself out of the room. And she was alone with Gavin.

He had removed his suit coat and tie. His pale yellow dress shirt and navy slacks were less formal, but no less attractive. In fact, he looked pretty darned good. Then she noticed his intense expression. M.J.

remembered it as the one he wore when he wanted something from her. She braced herself.

"I think you should move in," he said.

"Excuse me?" No amount of bracing would have prepared her for that.

"I want you to move in here. Work with Sean and maximize results."

The idea was preposterous on so many levels, she didn't know where to start. So she simply said, "No."

"Without even considering the offer?"

"Yes."

"Why?"

She blinked at him. "I don't have to explain my reasons."

"But it makes perfect sense," he argued.

"In what universe? I have a life. I have another job."

His mouth pulled tight for a moment. "Right."

She recognized this expression, too. It was the guarded one. The same one he'd had when he told her everyone has their price. "You're thinking it's about money."

"Isn't it?"

No, she wanted to scream. Her negative on moving in had come straight from the gut. She'd already broken her own unwritten rule and hugged Sean. On the surface that rule seemed heartless. For her it was survival. She couldn't get attached without reliving the loss of her own son. And what about Gavin hugging her? Hugs were supposed to give comfort; his offered something else. Something she didn't want to think about. She'd agreed to Sean's therapy, but she wouldn't agree to live under Gavin's roof.

She folded her arms over her chest. "From my perspective, you're the only one here who constantly obsesses over money."

He ran his fingers through his hair. "Forget I said that."

"Not likely."

"Let's look at this a different way."

"What other way?" she asked warily.

"You look tired, M.J. Believe me, I don't usually notice that sort of thing, but it's pretty obvious."

She was only surprised he'd picked up on it. After that initial adrenaline rush following Sean's breakthrough, she felt as if she didn't have the energy to put one foot in front of the other. But it was sort of humiliating that she looked so bad.

"It's time for me to go home," she said.

"If you moved in, you'd be home now. You wouldn't have to think about anything but working with Sean."

That's where he was wrong. Thinking about Gavin happened all the time. She didn't like it and moving in with him wasn't likely to make it go away.

"It's out of the question."

He let out a long breath. "Will you at least think about increasing your sessions with him?"

"You need to spend more time with your son."

"Agreed. And just one extra session a week might capitalize on this breakthrough and bring him back faster."

"I don't want to put too much pressure on him."

"You saw that he didn't want you to go." He met her gaze. "Is that pressure? He loves working with you."

Love? Interesting choice of words and a red flag for her. "I don't think so."

"One more hour. Is that too much to ask?"

He had no idea what he was asking. And it wasn't simply about the time involved. That was the least of her concerns.

When she didn't answer, his eyes glowed with challenge and something darker. "It's sixty minutes out of your week to give my son his life back. And I'll make it worth your while financially."

He'd had her before he mentioned money, but M.J. didn't want him to know that. He thought she was mercenary and it would be best to let him go on thinking that. It gave her a suit of armor, an umbrella of protection, a safe zone. She didn't want anything to do with personal. It already felt too personal with Gavin.

"All right," she said. "I'll give him one more hour a week."

Chapter Five

M.J. opened her eyes and winced at the bright light. A sharp pain shot straight through her head. When she touched a hand to her forehead, she felt a shockingly large bump. The attempt to sit up was unwise since a wave of dizziness took her back down again. Trying not to move, she glanced around at the beeping electronic equipment. There was an IV in her arm and circular sticky things on her chest with wires attached to the annoying beeping machine. She was in a bed, a very hard bed, in a semi-reclining position. There was a curtain pulled around her.

She had a vague memory of chaos. Then she'd been taken to a room where they slid her into a white-light tube. Sort of like being eaten by a doughnut. She recalled a whirring sound, being told to lie still. Now there was nothing vague about the fact that every muscle in her body ached.

Suddenly the curtain parted and her mother was hovering over her. "M.J.? You're awake. Thank God."

"Mom?" Her mouth was dry and her voice hoarse. "Where am I?"

"The ER."

"Why?" Duh. Now there was a dumb question when her hand was still gingerly testing the mountain-size bump on her head. But what put it there? She rephrased. "What happened?"

"You were in a car accident, M.J."

Oh, God. She couldn't remember being hit. "The other driver?"

"It was a single car accident."

M.J. couldn't seem to process what that meant, except that, thankfully, no one else had been hurt. She closed her eyes and found that helped the ache in her head. When she opened them again, she saw her mother smile.

"Hello, sleepyhead."

"Hmm?"

"You drifted off again."

Her head felt a little better. "What are you doing here?"

Evelyn reached over and squeezed her fingers. "They found my number in your purse and called me.

Aunt Lil is here, too, but they would only let one of us sit with you at a time. We've been taking turns."

Sit with her? M.J. shifted on the bed. "It wasn't necessary for you to come. I'm taking care of it."

Her mother's look was wry. "You were doing a fine job, too. Being unconscious and all."

"I'm awake now."

"So am I. And sleep won't be happening anytime soon. There's something about waiting for your child to get home, then finding out she was in a car accident."

"I'm sorry, Mom. But I feel fine," she lied. "We can go home now." She couldn't think about how much this was going to cost. The downside of substitute teaching was lack of medical benefits a full-time employee would receive.

"You'll go when the doctor says you can go. They want to keep you for observation. When someone loses consciousness, they need to make sure your brain's not scrambled."

Traumatic brain injury. Sean. Gavin. She remembered. Her brain was working just fine. "It's not scrambled."

"Good. But we'll wait until they release you." Her mother looked concerned; her hand was cold. "I was so worried when you didn't get home at the usual time. That car of yours is old and unreliable, not to mention the strain of that winding road to Cliff House. God only knows what could have happened. I called Gavin—"

"No. You didn't."

"Yes. I did."

"How?"

Again the wry, motherly look. "There's this lovely little invention called a telephone. I picked it up and pressed a couple of numbers and presto—he answered."

M.J. would have smiled, but it would have hurt. "That's not what I meant. How did you know his number?"

"You have his card tucked into the pocket on your desk blotter."

"Oh." M.J. sighed. "There was no reason to involve him."

"I wanted to know if you were still there. When he said you'd been gone and should have been home already, I got frantic. He offered to help." She smiled, although her blue eyes were still shadowed with concern. "He seems like a very nice man."

Probably he was. M.J. tried not to think about him. "I hope you called him back when you found out I was okay."

"Of course I did. I knew he'd want to know you'd been found. He insisted on coming to the hospital."

"You need to call him back and tell him that's not necessary." She was fine. Why in the world would he bother himself with her? For Sean. It would be about her work with his son. Professional worry. That should have made her feel better.

Evelyn sat on the bed. "I don't think he'll listen.

He's a take-charge sort of man, isn't he? I get the feeling he doesn't take no for an answer."

M.J. rolled her eyes and the movement hurt, but not quite as much as it had before. "That's putting it mildly. He runs his world with an iron hand."

"That's not necessarily a bad thing, you know."

It was when one disagreed with him. "He's a millionaire and they have different rules."

Evelyn shrugged. "That's probably true. But from the little you've said about him, there's a lot to respect. He got you back into the profession you love."

That wasn't about Gavin, but M.J. wasn't at liberty to say so. "He loves his son very much." There was something about a bump on the head. When the thought popped into her mind, M.J. blurted it out without engaging the filter to her mouth. "Why didn't I ever meet my father? Why didn't we ever talk about him?"

Evelyn sighed, then sat in the chair by the bed, still holding M.J.'s hand. "It was my mess to clean up. I didn't want to burden you with all of that. I just wanted to give you as normal a life as I possibly could."

"You did that, Mom."

M.J. wouldn't ever make her mother feel guilty. She'd done a good job. She'd provided a home, food, clothes. But M.J.'s family only consisted of her mother and Aunt Lil. Most kids had a two-parent home and M.J. had always felt different. Set apart. When she saw her friends with their fathers, she felt as if she were missing out on something important.

"I did my best." Her mother suddenly looked tired.

"No one could have asked more than that."

"The thing is, M.J., not all men are no-shows like your father. Vince was proof of that."

Yeah. Her husband had other flaws, but he'd definitely been around.

"And Gavin," her mother continued. "He's more proof that not all men are irresponsible jerks."

"I'm sure he has other flaws," M.J. said.

At that moment the privacy curtain swung sideways and the man in question stood there, flaws and all. Until that moment, M.J. hadn't noticed that it hurt to breathe.

Gavin stared at M.J., relieved that her eyes were open and she was talking. She had a nasty bump on her forehead. "Are you all right?" he demanded.

"Fine." She looked at her mother. "I thought you said I could only have one visitor at a time."

"That's what they told Lil and I," her mother confirmed, studying the man standing at the foot of the bed.

"I didn't ask permission."

"Why doesn't that surprise me?" M.J. looked annoyed—and vulnerable.

Gavin had never been one to follow the rules when they didn't suit him. He was accustomed to getting what he wanted and right now that was information about her condition.

Her sassiness was a relief. When he found out she'd been in an accident, he'd been worried.

He looked at her mother. "It's nice to see you again, Evelyn."

"And it's nice of you to come to the hospital."

"I was concerned." He glanced at M.J.

Evelyn stood up. "I'll just go let my sister know what's going on."

"Don't leave on my account," he said.

"Not a problem. Just in case they decide to enforce the one-visitor rule."

"Come back soon, Mom." M.J. clung to her mother's hand for several moments, then let go and the older woman disappeared around the curtain.

Gavin moved closer to the gurney and looked down. "Are you all right?" he asked again.

She nodded, then winced. "Just a bump on the head."

"Good thing it's hard."

"Hey," she protested. "No fair taking shots at me. I'm injured."

And she was lucky it wasn't worse, he thought. He'd passed the accident on his way to the hospital. Her banged-up little car was just being loaded onto a flatbed truck as he stopped. The cop on the scene had told him no other vehicles were involved and that M.J. had failed to maintain the lane, then apparently overcorrected and flipped. "You were lucky, M.J. The cops think you fell asleep at the wheel."

Gavin had seen M.J.'s exhaustion for himself and didn't know why she was pushing herself so hard. He'd almost succeeded in convincing himself not to feel guilty when he really looked at the lump on her forehead. Then he noticed the bruises just beginning to darken on her arms. Something tightened in his chest.

The hospital stirred up bad memories. His fear seeing Sean so small and helpless. Not moving. Not opening his eyes. Gavin hated hospitals. He hated the doctors speaking English, but having to translate everything.

And now he didn't much like himself for making the little bit of color she had left drain from M.J.'s face.

Clearly the situation was sinking in. What if she'd hit another car? Hurt someone else? What if it had happened on the winding road from Cliff House and her car picked up speed downhill before going over the side? She could have been killed. The knot inside him pulled tighter.

The hand she used to shield her eyes was trembling and showed off the IV. "The last thing I remember was being so tired I could hardly hold my head up."

He'd noticed. It was what had prompted him to ask her to move in. The words had barely left his mouth when he'd regretted them. Then he'd reminded himself his reasons were all about Sean. She was an employee; he signed her paycheck. It wasn't his responsibility to worry about her on a personal level. But he hadn't been able to help himself.

Because she'd looked so fragile.

Now she was injured.

"You can't go on like this." He wanted to say more, but it would sound harsh.

"I know." She took a deep, shuddering breath.

Just a few hours ago he'd badgered her into giving Sean another hour. In spite of her obvious fatigue and fragility. The thing was, Sean was making headway and Gavin was eager to build on the success. She'd refused to move in and he was accustomed to getting what he wanted. So he'd pushed. Her accident left him with no choice but to do it again.

"I think you should move into Cliff House."

She lowered her hand and met his gaze. "I hit my head, Gavin. That doesn't mean I don't remember. We've already been through this."

"I know." Impatience made his voice rougher than he intended when he recalled her words. "You have another job."

"Yes."

He didn't care that she taught other kids. He could only think about his own. Every time he wanted something from M.J., she dug in her heels until he sweetened the offer. It was hard not to put her in the same category as Sean's conniving mother.

But he'd seen M.J. with his son. He'd seen her face when Sean put his arms up for a hug. Gavin had felt her hesitation. And he'd clearly recognized the stark pain in her eyes when she'd gathered the child close and returned the embrace. Whatever she thought, her maternal instincts were not broken. She was warm and nurturing. And the sight of her with his child had exposed deep regrets. Sure, Gavin gave his child everything money could buy.

But he couldn't buy a mother's love for Sean.

"Like I said, you can't go on like this," he said.

"I can." She pushed aside the sheet covering her legs and struggled to sit up. In the thin, shapeless hospital gown, she seemed hardly more than a child. "All I need is a day or two. I just need to get out of here."

Gavin gently urged her back down and settled the sheet over her. "You'll get out of here when they say you're ready and not before."

There was a troubled look in her eyes. "I'm ready now. I can't afford—"

He touched a finger to her mouth to silence her. The softness of her lips caused a prickle of awareness that he quickly pushed away. "Not until the doctor releases you," he warned. Her only response was a glare. "And you're not going to distract me. We need to talk about your schedule."

"Summer will be here in about six weeks. I can hang on that long."

"What if you can't? What if you have another accident? Or get sick? What if you decide you have to give up something? I won't let it be Sean."

"You're wrong, Gavin. I won't—"

"You reached him. Don't pull him to the top of the mountain, show him the great view, then push him back down."

"I wouldn't do that. I'll make it work."

"The only way you can do that is by moving in with me. With Sean," he amended.

She shook her head. "That doesn't work for me."

"What if I pay you what you're making at both jobs?"

Her eyes widened. For someone who was quick with a comeback, she was uncharacteristically quiet. It could be the bump on the head, but he'd bet she was calculating just how generous the offer was.

Gavin didn't care about the money. She might be working him for as much as she could get, but it made no difference. His son had said "Daddy" and you couldn't put a price on that. She was getting results and she could be bought. He wouldn't trust her; he wouldn't allow himself to see her vulnerability.

He wouldn't let her smile get to him.

"I need an answer, M.J."

"I don't know what to say," she admitted. She put a hand to her forehead again and her mouth pulled tight as if she were in pain.

He couldn't afford to care. He was pushing, but it wasn't as if the arrangement wouldn't be better for her. It was for her own good.

"The offer is more than fair," he insisted.

"I know."

"Is that a yes?"

She met his gaze and whispered, "Yes."

"Good."

It was a win-win situation. He helped her; she helped Sean. A business arrangement. As long as he paid for her services, it wouldn't be personal.

Chapter Six

A week wasn't long enough to get used to being here, in this house.

M.J. had wondered and worried about meeting her financial obligations when summer came and substitute teaching wasn't an option. Full-time teachers were given the first opportunity for summer school positions. This situation was the answer to her prayer—and then again it wasn't. The previous schedule had given her a breather from the pain of seeing this little boy.

Now it took everything she had for M.J. to kneel beside Sean at the coffee table in the family room. The child, smelling sweet from his bath and now in his pajamas, was drawing before he went to bed.

Behind them, Gavin sat on the sofa. He'd changed from his suit and tie into jeans and a T-shirt. The cream color set off his tanned skin and dark eyes. And the denim did things to his thighs and butt that should be declared illegal. She *noticed*. Because she was still breathing. And she was a woman.

But the casual clothes didn't fool her. He had his laptop and the steady click of the keys told her he was working.

After the accident, she'd notified the school district that she wouldn't be available to substitute. Then she began living at Cliff House, a relief to her mother. M.J. wished she felt the same, but she was uneasy.

How stupid was that? She couldn't ask for more beautiful surroundings and Sean was her only responsibility. They spent time on his therapy and M.J. was in touch with his teacher, the two of them coordinating efforts to keep the boy as close to his grade level in school as possible. His attention span was short and when he got restless, M.J. would take him outside to run in the yard or down the wooden walkway to the beach where the two of them played in the sand.

But she felt Gavin's presence even when he wasn't there. And the three of them together in the family room felt—intimate. They didn't call it a family room for nothing. Except the three of them *weren't* family.

Back at her own home, a mountain of bills piled up. Glancing around Cliff House's elegantly decorated, spacious family room, M.J. felt as if she was running away from her mess. Possibly into another one with another man because every nerve she had seemed to merge into one and Gavin was getting on it.

. But she was between a rock and a hard place. Out of the frying pan, into the fire. Or any other cliché she could throw at the fact that Gavin was paying her well and living here was the best solution she had. For now.

A fist squeezed her heart at the sight of Sean's freckle-splashed nose and the dark lashes. She looked at his drawing and saw that it was three stick figures. The tallest and shortest had black hair, the one in the middle yellow. The heads were disproportionately large, but that was normal for a six-year-old.

"Who's this?" she asked.

"Daddy."

M.J. looked over her shoulder at the man behind them who didn't look up from his laptop. Since she'd been here, Gavin had made it home in time for dinner only twice. When he was around, he spent time in his office or as he was now—here, but not here. Even so, with every day that passed, she found herself awaiting Gavin's arrival just a bit more, her heart beating just a little faster at the sight of him.

She touched the middle figure with yellow hair and asked, "And this?" When Sean pointed at her, she said, "M.J."

He grinned, then went back to concentrating on his people. Finally he let out a very big sigh and put his pencil down, and she knew he was finished. He handed the picture to her.

She studied it, noting that he'd drawn fingers, toes and eyelashes on each of them. The amount of detail was a good sign. Putting an arm across his shoulders, she squeezed. It constituted a hug. That wall had come down and now hugs came spontaneously. Because he needed it and she couldn't help herself.

"This is a very good job, Sean. High five." She held up her hand and he slapped it, a big grin lighting his face. They were working on "thank you." But not at the moment.

Then he jumped up and grabbed the drawing. He crawled up onto the couch beside his father, bumping Gavin's arm.

"Careful, buddy. This is work," he said absently.

Sean thrust the drawing underneath his father's nose, between him and the computer screen.

"Nice picture, Sean." Gavin barely looked before setting the paper aside.

When Sean started to scramble across Gavin's lap to retrieve it, he grabbed him. "This is very important, Sean. Play with M.J."

Gavin wasn't looking when Sean's mouth pulled tight. Or when the little boy pointed to his picture and held up his hand.

"Daddy." The tone was loud, the way only a six-year-old could say it, so that everyone in the next county could hear.

"Yes, son?"

But Gavin didn't look up until the boy put his little hand on the broad shoulder and pushed as hard as he could. "What?" he asked, distracted.

"Daddy." Sean held up his hand again and pointed to it.

When his father still didn't look up, the boy started to close the laptop. Gavin held it open. "Don't, son. I need this for tomorrow."

The therapist in M.J. knew she should stand back, allow Sean to get his point across and Gavin to deal with the situation. But she wasn't feeling like a therapist at the moment. The mother in her wanted the man flogged for his indifference.

"One minute, Sean," Gavin said.

M.J. stood. "He wants you to give him a high five."

Surprise flickered in Gavin's eyes, but he didn't say anything. He picked up the drawing and looked at it, then slapped a high five into his son's little hand. "Good job."

Sean grinned, then slid down from the couch and skipped across the room to a cupboard beside the big-screen TV. After opening it, he pulled out his favorite dinosaur game and brought it back to Gavin, jostling him when he put it on the sofa.

Gavin shook his head. "I can't, buddy."

The child did a little-boy roar, indicating he wanted his father to play the game. Apparently he had inherited the can't-take-no-for-an-answer gene.

When Gavin looked up from his laptop, he shook his head. "I think it's time for bed, son."

Sean shook his head.

"Yes. Now." Gavin's tone was firm. "Go brush your teeth."

The little boy's hands curled into fists while mutiny flared in his eyes. But he did as he was told.

M.J. waited until she was sure the child was out of earshot, roughly the equivalent of counting to ten. Her philosophy was to never miss an opportunity for learning to happen and it was time for Gavin to learn a thing or two. "I think it's time you got a demonstration of some therapy techniques."

Gavin looked up, his expression bland. "Isn't that what I'm paying you for?"

"Oh, I forgot. I'm part of the child-rearing team who punches a time card." Sometimes sarcasm could get his attention. "The thing is, Gavin, a paid employee can only do so much."

"What does that mean?" He set the laptop on the coffee table beside the colored pencils scattered there. Then he met her gaze.

Without thinking, she sat down beside him, so close her jeans brushed his. She swore she saw sparks and hoped it was nothing more than static electricity. Trying to look as if she was adjusting her position, she scooted further away.

"What I mean is," she started. "there's an undefined emotional component in recovery from traumatic brain injury. A therapist can suggest techniques and guide the process, but for the child, it's family that provides the driving force."

"I believe I provided that when I convinced you to work with Sean."

"I'm not his parent."

"No." Gavin's mouth thinned. "I am. His *single* father. I have other responsibilities. To my company and employees. I have to earn a living. And you're sounding suspiciously judgmental."

She wanted to say "bite me" but took a deep breath. "If anyone understands earning a living, it's me." And she worked very hard to put the overwhelming responsibilities out of her mind. "But that doesn't mean that when he does something he's proud of you can't give him a hug. A word or two of praise. Play with him for a few minutes. Read him a story. Any man can be a father, but it takes a little something more to be a dad."

"I wouldn't know. The boarding school I went to was fresh out of fathers," he snapped. "But it got the job done."

Raw emotion darkened his features. She doubted he knew it was there, but it gave her a glimpse of the lonely little boy he must have been. The look reminded her of Sean and tugged at her heart. "What about your mother?"

"He divorced her."

Like so many kids, he was a product of a broken home. He was right. She was being judgmental without knowing the facts. But the cycle couldn't be broken until shortcomings were pointed out and acknowledged. And there was another child who would fall victim to the cycle if she took the easy way out and kept her mouth shut.

"It's true that parenting is a job, the hardest one there is. But outsourcing all of it isn't the best option."

"Couldn't prove that by me," he said. "I turned out okay. Which is fortunate as my father didn't tolerate failure."

That explained a lot. He had no role model for being a father. But her training was all about changing patterns and making new, positive ones. She didn't work at his company, but he'd reminded her she was an employee—one who was very close to crossing the line. But she had to try.

"Since moving in I've been able to observe the father-son dynamic and something occurred to me."

"What would that be?"

"Sean had a pretty significant breakthrough when you walked in the door. I don't think that's coincidence."

"No?" He looked skeptical.

She linked her hands in her lap. "Gavin, you're the most important person in his world. He wants to please you. He's going to work harder for you than for anyone else."

He settled his arm along the top of the sofa, his fingers inches from her shoulder, his eyes narrowed. "Since you're the queen of parenting advice, you must have had a perfect childhood."

M.J. didn't let the edge in his tone intimidate her. She also didn't point out that he was deliberately changing the subject because she'd probably said too much already. "There's no such thing as perfect. But I never knew my father. Which means I wasn't striving to please him. It also means I had different issues."

Questions swirled in his eyes. "Speaking of issues, you were married, but you use your mother's last name. Why is that?"

The question took her by surprise, which was the only reason the next words slipped out. "My husband and I shared a bed and a child—and I didn't really know him at all."

"Does he have anything to do with why you nearly killed yourself working two jobs?"

For a man who seemed to ignore so much around him, he was far too perceptive. That didn't mean he was entitled to an answer. The whole ugly mess was far too humiliating. It wasn't easy to admit she'd been so stupid and she'd needed the two jobs to clean up after herself. But Gavin wasn't the type to be easily put off.

She came up with an explanation as close to the truth as possible. "The house needs work. Plumbing. Electrical. A roof. Cosmetic stuff. The contractor gave me an estimate that looked like the national debt."

"Ouch." He nodded with understanding. "You could take out a loan against the property."

Her husband had already done that to finance his gambling problem, she thought grimly. "I'd rather not go that route."

He nodded. "You can negotiate with them. Work out payments for each phase."

She hadn't thought of it. One just did what one was told. It hadn't occurred to her to call the loan company and negotiate the debt. "I'll do that. Thanks for the suggestion."

"You're welcome. I may not win Father of the Year, but business I'm good at."

"You love your son, Gavin. No one could doubt that. And it's the most important thing." She sighed. "You'll have to teach me how not to be scared of the building contractor. I keep picturing a black-haired man twisting his oily mustache and laughing glee-fully as he plots to separate me from my money."

"On that cheerful note, I think I'll go say good night to Sean."

He grinned and the look seared her inside, warming a frozen, lifeless place. An angry Gavin she could go toe-to-toe with. She could put him on the same list of men who let her down along with her father, her husband. But this kinder, gentler Gavin scared her.

She stood abruptly. "I think I'll take my walk now."

It felt like escape when she hurried through the house to the front door. Outside, the air was moist and smelled of the sea, and she breathed deeply. This evening exercise had become a ritual, to clear her head. But she was afraid it wouldn't work this time. She wanted to run away from it all—this house. Sean. Gavin. But she needed this job.

And, she suspected, Gavin needed her. To remind him that what his son needed most didn't cost anything but his time.

* * *

After another long week, Gavin walked into the house from the garage and, before going in search of Sean, dropped his briefcase in his office. Glancing out the French doors, he saw that it was still light outside. He wasn't used to getting home when it was light. But he'd canceled himself out of the R & D meeting and told himself it had nothing to do with M.J.

He hadn't stuck his son in boarding school; he wasn't like his father.

And he hadn't meant to tell her about that, except somehow she'd gotten to him. For future reference, he shouldn't continue a discussion with M. J. Taylor when he was too angry to think straight.

When Gavin left his office, he listened. It didn't occur to him that he'd grown accustomed to the sound of her voice and his son's laughter until he didn't hear either. The house was too quiet.

He walked into the family room, expecting to see them working on a puzzle or playing a game. He found M.J., sitting on the sofa, the recliner extended. When she didn't react to him, he moved closer and saw that her eyes were closed. The dark circles underneath her eyes stood out in contrast to her pale skin.

Bruises from her accident had finally faded. Since the day he'd tracked her down at the high school, her face had been in various stages of healing. Life knocked her around. And the cryptic remark about her husband told him she'd had more than just the recent blows. The look on her face had been all about pain with anger mixed in. And disillusionment.

Their conversation had stirred his curiosity. But that wasn't why he'd come home early, either.

He stared at her long dark lashes, delicate cheekbones, full lips, slender throat. As far as he could tell, she didn't wear makeup, but her skin was soft and flawless. Since moving in, her work attire had consisted of blue jeans and T-shirts—the better to work with Sean. Today her cotton blouse was a pale blue that he knew would accentuate her eyes—when they were open. As she dozed, her chest rose and fell gently, drawing his attention to the curve of her breasts and the flare of her hips.

How could he have ever thought her plain? The more he got to know her, the more it became apparent that her appeal wasn't obvious. Her beauty was subtle and crept up on a man, which made her more dangerous.

Her lashes fluttered then lifted and she blinked at him. "Gavin." She sat up and looked around, as if she didn't know where she was.

Apparently she'd been sleeping hard, he thought. "Hi."

"Hi. What are you doing here?"

"I live here?" he said, his mouth curving up.

She smiled. "I meant, it's early and you're home."

It wasn't criticism because she was still too sleepy to consciously get on his case. But he still felt a twinge and wondered why he'd tolerated her comment on his parenting skills. Probably because a lot of what she'd said made sense. God knows he'd worked his ass off to please his own father. Without success.

"Where's Sean?"

"I wish you'd called." She looked disappointed. "Henderson and Lenore took him to a movie."

"Oh."

"It's their afternoon off."

He'd forgotten. "I see."

"Sean was really restless and we agreed that an outing would be a positive distraction for him."

"Good."

"They made me stay home," she explained.

"I don't see any ropes, chains or shackles," he said, sliding his hands in his pockets as he studied her.

She looked sheepish. "Is that your way of telling me I'm stubborn and don't take suggestions gracefully?"

"Yeah."

"Okay." She smiled. "They said I looked tired and needed a break."

They were right, he thought, his gaze lingering on the shadows beneath her eyes. That's why he noticed when her eyes widened in surprise.

"Gavin, you didn't come home early to work with Sean, did you?"

"No. It was just one of those days—"

"Oh." Disappointment took the sparkle out of her. "But we can still use the time. I can show you some stuff. He'll be back in a little while and you can work with him."

"That's all right. You can—"

But she was already moving across the room, to the cupboard beside the television. She pulled out a stack of items and brought them to the coffee table, then knelt down.

Patting the carpet beside her, she said, "You have to get down to his level." Then she noticed his slacks. "Probably you'll want to wear something more comfortable."

Slip into something more comfortable. Although he knew that's not what she meant, it's where his testosterone took him. And that was damned annoying. He'd hired her because she'd come highly recommended. The fact that he'd originally found her plain had been a bonus. Now the rules seemed to be changing on him.

But he knelt beside her and stared at the pile of games, blocks, puzzles and books. "These look like toys."

Her mouth curved into a soft smile. "You're brighter than the average bear. It's why they pay you the big bucks."

He couldn't help smiling back. "And I'm paying you the big bucks to play with him—why?"

Instead of taking offense, she grinned. "Because I know *how* to play."

"Show me." Again his double-crossing thoughts took a sensuous turn. His voice had a rasp to it and he hoped she didn't notice. Why the hell was he twisting every innocent thing she said into something seductive? Beware of game-playing women who only wanted money. That was a rule carved in the stone of his heart.

"It's important to find out what the individual child likes. In Sean's case, I knew the first time I met him that he was into dinosaurs."

"Yeah. Since he was about three," Gavin confirmed.

"So I made flash cards of them. And cars and zoo animals." She held up cardboard squares with words handwritten on them. "I call this the copycat game. I say the word and he repeats it. We're working on reading, speaking and memory at the same time. My goal is to get him to remember several words and string them into a sentence. That's what the game of three was all about."

He pulled a container of blocks from the stack. "And these? I'm not the sort of man who argues with results. But when I look at this it screams toy."

"Part of memory exercises." She dumped them on the floor. "I put three or four in a configuration." She leaned forward and her hair swung in a golden curtain over her cheek. She stacked the bold yellow, bright blue and vivid red blocks, then swept her hand across and destroyed it. Grinning, she said, "He loves that part."

"Then what?" he asked, pulling his gaze from her smile.

"The objective is for him to remember the pattern and reproduce it. Again it's all about recall. Stringing blocks and putting words together. Believe it or not, this will help him with his word patterns."

Gavin absently stacked the blocks. Occupying his hands with the wooden triangles, squares and oblongs because his fingers tingled with the urge to tuck her hair behind her ear. "What else?"

She pulled a game out from the stack. "This is a language-based game. There are clues—visual and auditory. He guesses who or where."

"I see." He liked the sound of her voice, so soft and patient.

"There are tons of activities he can do. And the strategy is basically the same—repetition of directions and situations for practice. Breaking things down into steps, using visual cues—pictures, words, symbols."

Visual. Auditory. Using the senses. Gavin's senses were filled with the sight, sound and scent of her. "I see."

"He gets frustrated because he can't say what he wants. I read lists of words to him, to help improve his vocabulary. He repeats them one at a time. We're working up to phrases, then typical sentences. Like 'See the car.' Then I'll add adjectives. 'See the blue car.' Then, 'See the blue car in the garage.'"

Her enthusiasm was contagious and he felt himself pulled in like driftwood in an undertow. So he deliberately sifted through the mound of material. The games, blocks and cards—touching them because he badly wanted to touch her.

"At first I was giving Sean a lot of assistance," she continued earnestly. "But he's making progress, Gavin."

His name on her lips made him look into her eyes. Big mistake. "Is he?"

She nodded, enthusiasm and passion on her face. "He's becoming more independent with each skill we work on."

He could see why Sean had so much fun with her. He recalled the two of them laughing as Sean drew his picture. Wisps of memories of his own mother seemed just out of reach and an emptiness opened up inside him. She'd left his father and the old man had said all she'd wanted was the Spencer money, so he'd paid her off and she hadn't come back. The next thing Gavin knew, he'd been shipped off to boarding school.

Loneliness settled over him now the way it had then. He'd hated it there and that was why he'd been determined Sean would never feel that way. But it wasn't enough. Gavin couldn't give him a mother.

He stood. "I get the drift."

"You should know how to explain what you want to accomplish. I can give you examples of how to get everything across to him as honestly and concretely as possible."

"I have work to do."

Confusion clouded her eyes. "But you're home early. He'll be back soon."

What he had to do was get away from M.J. She made him think about things. The past. The present.

Kissing her. Things that he didn't want to think about. He needed to escape because he'd enjoyed talking to her. He'd noticed her as a woman and it wasn't the first time. But mostly he didn't want to get used to needing her.

For Sean's sake, he hoped progress was happening. And for himself? Definitely. He wanted M.J.'s work here to be done.

Chapter Seven

"Sean will be down in a minute." Gavin stood on the other side of the kitchen island. "It's good of you to volunteer for chef duty."

"Chef?" She measured pancake mix, then poured it in the bowl. It was Saturday morning and he wasn't going to the office. The light yellow cotton shirt and jeans were a clue. And she'd wished she'd thought it through before she'd opened her big mouth and offered. "I'm not the high-white-hat type."

His forehead wrinkled as he thought for a moment. "Since clothes don't make the man, I'm going to guess chef's threads or lack thereof don't necessarily mean one can't cook."

"Yagottawanna."

"Excuse me?"

His confusion made her laugh. "That's what I said when my aunt threw that one at me."

"Care to explain?"

It seemed ages ago, but had only been about twelve weeks. Right after she'd met Gavin. "Not long ago, my aunt Lil made the best pot of pea soup on the planet." She shot him a warning look when he started to open his mouth. "Don't go there. Tasting every pot of pea soup on the planet is not a prerequisite for knowing my aunt makes the best."

"Say that five times fast," he said wryly.

"Right. Anyway, my mother said that being a single mom, she hadn't had time to nurture her inner chef."

"Because your dad wasn't around."

"Right." She couldn't believe she'd told him that. It wouldn't have happened if she wasn't living under his roof. And she wouldn't be here if he hadn't worn her down at a particularly vulnerable moment. But she knew better than to let it happen again. "Anyway, Aunt Lil says some people cook because they have to, and any fool who can read can follow a recipe. To others it's a calling and working with food is exciting and fun."

"Which group do you fall into?"

"The fool with the recipe," she said, reading the pancake mix box. "And I'm a little out of practice."

"Because your aunt does the cooking at home?"

She nodded. "Mom and I are grateful."

"Do you miss them?" he asked.

She thought about that and the fact that she stopped by every couple days for her mail. God forbid she should miss seeing the stack of bills. And she talked to her family on the phone every day. "No," she finally said.

He nodded. "That's good. And I appreciate you filling in."

"We all have to make sacrifices. Yours will happen when you taste this. I haven't made pancakes for a long time. You may want to take back your gratitude."

"I doubt it. Henderson and Lenore don't often ask for time off."

"They seem dedicated." She cracked an egg and dropped it into the dry mix, then poured in milk.

"Yeah. They always try to give me warning. I have to make child-care arrangements. This was unexpected, but I like to accommodate them whenever possible. I'm glad you're here."

"Me, too."

M.J. had seen the older couple's excitement when their daughter called with the pregnancy news. They couldn't have been more delighted. She wondered what it would feel like to not have mixed feelings about a baby on the way. She wouldn't know, as her pregnancy had been unplanned. Then she'd married Vince because she was pregnant and it seemed like the best solution. The biggest messes in her life were on account of men.

She met Gavin's gaze and steeled herself against

the twinkle in his eyes. "It's not every day you find out your daughter is having a baby. If they didn't go to Los Angeles to see the first-time parents-to-be, it would be a code violation."

"Code?" He leaned his forearms on the island's black-granite countertop.

"Grandparents' code of conduct," she explained, beating the mixture in the bowl with a wire whisk.

"Ah." He sat down on one of the stools at the island. "Are there a lot of rules?"

M.J. figured if his own father shipped him off to boarding school, the man almost certainly hadn't won Grandfather of the Year award. Gavin was a paradox. On the one hand, he provided his son with the best care and loved him very much. On the other hand, the bits and pieces he'd revealed about his childhood convinced her he wasn't being a jerk when he put his son second. He simply didn't have a father's skills because he hadn't had a father. He'd been raised in boarding school—raised by staff. Sean lived at home and went to regular school, but Gavin was exhibiting the same behavior he'd learned from his own father.

She hated that she could see both sides of him because she just wanted to think he was a jerk.

"Not too many rules," she finally answered. "Spoiling is not only allowed, it's mandatory. Failure to complete that assignment will be dealt with severely."

"I see. Anything else?"

She stopped mixing the batter as she thought. "They might be hitting you up for a raise."

"Oh?"

"Buying all those toys a child will never play with gets pretty expensive."

"I'll keep that in mind." He grinned.

M.J. felt a flutter in her chest and knew it was her body's reaction to this man. There was just a kitchen island between them and she wished it was a state the size of Texas. She hadn't anticipated being a good Samaritan and offering to fill in for the older couple would entail talking with and teasing Gavin Spencer while she cooked.

With the bowl of batter in hand, she walked to the stove and turned on the heat. Gavin should know all about turning up the heat because he was sure turning up hers. "So, what are you and Sean doing today?"

"I promised him a picnic on the beach."

She glanced at him over her shoulder. Had he actually listened to her? Was this about her telling him to pay attention to his son? To not outsource fatherhood? Later, she couldn't believe she'd had the nerve to say that. In fact it hadn't been nerve at all. Just another example of her leading with her heart for Sean's sake. Another instance of not thinking something through. If she had, she probably wouldn't have risked this job.

The good thing was that since the words had popped out of her mouth, Gavin had seemed to make an effort. He'd come home early and now he was planning an outing with his son. A little glow started inside her, a good feeling.

Then the son in question raced into the room, his little freckled face shining. "Daddy—"

Gavin looked down and grinned, then grabbed the child and settled him on his lap. "Hey, buddy."

"Beach."

"That's right. We're going to the beach for a picnic."

"Play." The child looked at him expectantly.

Gavin nodded. "We can play ball. What about playing with your Frisbee?"

Sean nodded. "Catch."

"Okay. We can bring the baseball and gloves, too." He settled his big hand on the boy's shoulder. "M.J.'s making pancakes. Are you hungry?"

Sean nodded.

"Okay, then," she said. "Coming right up."

She dripped a tiny bit of batter on the skillet to test the heat. When it sizzled, she concentrated on cooking and half listened to the guys behind her. Sean's giggling was a happy sound and she couldn't help smiling.

"Okay, I think these are ready." She'd already put out three sets of silverware and carried the stacked plates to the oak table in the nook. "Eat up before they get cold."

Sean scrambled up into his chair, then struggled to pour the maple syrup. Knowing he was going to drown the pancakes, M.J. watched.

Gavin was several steps behind her and saw when it was too late. "Whoa, buddy," he said, and grabbed the bottle.

"Me," Sean said, reaching for it.

"No. That's enough." Gavin met her gaze and a gleam of understanding stole into his eyes. "You knew that was going to happen."

"It was more of a sneaking suspicion with undertones of an educated guess."

"You could have stepped in."

"I could have been wrong." It was the school of hard knocks method of learning. She shrugged. "There's plenty of batter. I'll make more."

"Good plan." When his cell phone rang, he answered. "Spencer."

Even with her back turned, M.J. knew from his end of the conversation that it was the office calling and something important required his attention. When another stack of pancakes was ready, she brought it to the table. With his phone wedged between ear and shoulder, Gavin put two on Sean's plate and helped with the syrup. The child took a big bite, but while he was chewing, there was a worried look on his face as he watched his father.

Gavin snapped the phone closed and blew out a long breath. He looked at her and she knew what was coming.

"Sean, Daddy has to go to work."

"No." The boy shook his head as his happy expression vanished into stubborn.

"I'm sorry, buddy. There's a problem only Daddy can fix."

"No." This time he shouted the word.

"I won't be gone long, Seanster. We can still go to the beach later. It will just take a little while."

Sean threw his fork. "No."

"Don't throw things," Gavin ordered.

The little boy pushed his plate and it would have slid onto the floor if M.J. hadn't caught it.

"Behave yourself." Gavin gave him a stern look.

Sean pointed at him. "Stay."

"I can't, Sean. It's work."

Sean slid off his chair and pushed it. When he started to give it another shove, Gavin was there, down on one knee in front of the child. The boy made a fist and hit him in the chest.

"Sean, go to your room."

M.J. knew this time she had to get involved. It wasn't about indifference on Gavin's part. This was impulse control and frustration related to the brain injury. The behavior needed to be dealt with and sending him to his room wouldn't help. She took Sean by the upper arms and turned him to face her, holding him firmly. "No hitting. Use words, Sean. Remember. Mad. Sad. Glad."

"Daddy." The little boy struggled against being restrained. "Stay."

"Your father has to go to work. He'll be back in a little while. How does that make you feel?"

Dark eyes so like Gavin's filled with anger. "Mad."

She felt the little body vibrating with anger. "Daddy doesn't want to go to work, but he has to. So he can buy you dinosaurs."

"Rex."

She nodded as she rubbed her hands soothingly up and down his arms. "Yes, the T Rex."

"Tops," the little boy said.

"Triceratops," she corrected.

He pointed to Gavin. "Play."

"Daddy has to do his job and sometimes that means he can't play. Just like you have to do school-work. If Daddy doesn't work, he can't buy you pancakes or toys. It's not okay to hit or throw things. You need to tell Daddy that you're sorry."

The little boy shook his head and twisted to break her grip. She held him firmly. Apparently he wasn't quite over his mad yet. She'd been through this kind of behavior with him before. In addition to his looks, Sean had inherited determination from his father and it was a very deep gene pool.

She met the boy's angry gaze. "We're going to stay here until you tell Daddy you're sorry for hitting him."

Sean shook his head, but she could tell the rage was weakening.

"Look at Daddy, Sean." She turned him toward his father. "I know you didn't mean to hurt Daddy."

The little shoulders rose, then fell as the fight drained out of him. He let out a big sigh. "Sorry."

Gavin brushed a hand over his hair. "It's okay, Seanster. I'm sorry, too. We'll go to the beach later." When he looked at her there was admiration as well as a question in his eyes. "That was impressive. How did you do that?"

She shrugged. "I'm bigger."

He smiled. "No, really."

"It's not hard. You have to pick the important hills to die on, then show up for the battle. Respect is worth taking a stand on and I was prepared to stand as long as it took."

"There's a crisis at the office. I wouldn't go if I didn't have to."

She wasn't walking in his shoes and didn't know what constituted a crisis in his world. She understood that he hadn't been exposed to the skills he would need as a parent but when would Sean come first? She'd defended him to his son because Sean needed to respect authority. It didn't mean she condoned Gavin's decision to break his word.

And she especially didn't want to see both sides of the situation.

Because a short time ago she'd talked and laughed with him over pancake batter. Attraction to Gavin was a given, what with his movie star good looks. But she was finding that there were other things about him she could like, and she didn't want to like him.

That was a whole level of messy that she didn't want or need. What was the point of painful lessons if you didn't learn anything and made the same mistake?

M.J. couldn't believe this was the same child who'd had a meltdown not long ago. He'd been expecting a picnic and she gave him one. After packing sandwiches, fruit and drinks in a cooler, she'd changed into shorts and a tank top and walked with Sean down the wooden stairs to the beach below Cliff House.

The warm sand caressed her feet. The hot sun felt good on her shoulders and made her glad she'd slathered them with sunblock. There was just the right amount of sea breeze for maximum comfort. The sky was a cloudless blue and the ocean sparkled like diamonds. Sean had carted the toys he'd wanted to bring with him and dropped them in a heap before helping her spread a sheet out to sit on.

As if that was going to happen, what with his high level of get-up-and-go. They were kneeling close to where the ocean's waves lapped against the shore, the hard-packed wet sand. Where if you dug just a little, you hit water and a handful drizzled into a free-form sand sculpture. She looked at Sean's smiling face. He was overflowing with sweetness, energy and good humor.

And Gavin was missing it.

Not her problem, she reminded herself. Therapy was her responsibility and she couldn't miss an opportunity now.

M.J. picked up a thin piece of driftwood and drew in the sand. S-E-A-N.

The child looked at it, smiled and pointed to the T Rex on the shirt over his chest.

"Yes, you," she said. "Sean."

She brushed the letters away, then dragged the stick through the sand again. S-e-e S-e-a-n p-l-a-y.

"See." He frowned as he studied it. "Play."

"Yes. We're playing." She sighed.

She drew a heart in the wet sand, then handed Sean the stick. "You write something."

He looked thoughtful. Then he carved letters in the sand. D-a-d-y. A common enough misspelling for his age, but she got the drift.

"I know, kiddo."

He looked at her, then printed two more letters below the first word. M-J.

Her heart squeezed painfully. So much for her resolve not to bond with a child again.

"House," he said, holding out the yellow bucket.

"You want to build a house in the sand?" she asked, emotion making her voice tremble. But the moment was broken and she was glad.

"M.J.," he said, pointing to her. "Build."

"Sand isn't really my medium. I'm better with words."

"Build," he ordered.

Anything other than making a mound of sand was beyond her sand construction capabilities. "How about a peanut butter and jelly sandwich first?"

He nodded enthusiastically. "Juice."

"You bet. I had a feeling you were thirsty and hungry."

When they stood and turned, she saw Gavin. Neither of them had heard him approach but he was here, hands on lean hips, looking at the heart carved in the sand. M.J. felt her pulse speed up. It was similar to the zing from a cup of coffee, but she knew the reaction had nothing to do with caffeine and everything to do with the brooding expression in his eyes. It was disconcerting to know that he didn't have to be smiling to affect her.

Sean looked up and grinned. "Daddy!"

Apparently all was forgiven. But with Gavin's pattern of putting Sean second most of the time, how long would it be before the child showed the scars?

She tucked a strand of hair behind her ear. "Hi. Is the crisis averted?"

"For now." He slid his fingertips into the pockets of his jeans. "Mind if I join you?"

She slid him a wry look. "Speaking as the queen of parenting advice, I'm all for you and Sean spending time together."

"Is there a PB&J in there for me?"

"You like that?"

He nodded. "Does anything taste better at the beach?"

She was surprised that a millionaire's tastes ran to the mundane. She'd have pictured him the wine and exotic cheese type. "I'm sure we can stretch the provisions to include you."

Gavin sat and Sean plopped himself in his father's lap while M.J. doled out sandwiches, drinks and chips. They ate in silence. When M.J. felt it stretch on too long, she searched for something to say.

"You arrived just in the nick of time," she said.

"Oh?"

"Sean wants to build a house."

"Is that a problem?"

"Yes, actually. My creative ability stops with piling sand into a mound."

He took a bite of his sandwich. "Then you can be the manual labor."

"Excuse me?"

"Sean and I will carve out the house and grounds while you keep us supplied with materials."

"Such as?"

"Sand and water," he said.

"Build?" Sean said, looking up.

"As soon as you finish eating," Gavin confirmed.

Sean gobbled up his sandwich, took a half sip from his boxed juice, then jumped up and took off for the water's edge.

Gavin looked after him, a rueful expression on his face. "I'd give anything if I could bottle that energy."

She'd give anything if Brian…

That stopped her. She'd been so caught up with Sean and everything going on, she hadn't realized it had been a while since she'd been consumed with memories of her loss. Her thoughts had been wrapped up in another little boy, one who needed more than therapy.

And they'd been wrapped up in that boy's father. Who had a smile that promised he could make her feel tugs and pulls she'd been so certain she was immune to.

M.J. wasn't sure which one—Gavin or Sean—was the most dangerous to her heart. Which was why she made up a stupid excuse and walked away.

Chapter Eight

Since this afternoon on the beach, Gavin had been waiting for a chance to speak to M.J. alone and he got it when she went on her evening walk. Sean was upstairs with Lenore supervising bath time and when he was ready for bed, Gavin would say good night.

As he walked down the stairs to the beach, he saw her standing by the ocean, the stiff breeze blowing her shoulder-length blond hair. Her jeans hugged the curve of her hips and shapely legs as her bare toes curled into the sand. Something tugged at him. There was something sad about the slender, solitary figure staring at the waves rushing ashore as high tide approached.

The sun was about thirty minutes from setting

and nature's ball of fire had turned the day's blue sky into pinkish-gold perfection.

Gavin jogged through the soft sand and stopped beside her. "Hi."

She jumped and put a hand to her chest. "You startled me."

"Sorry." The sound of the waves must have muffled his approach. His shoulder brushed hers as he folded his arms over his chest and stared at the ocean. "Nice night."

"Yes. But there's no such thing as a bad night, or day for that matter, when you live at the beach."

He'd never thought about that. "I guess I take it for granted."

"Anyone who doesn't appreciate the glory of that setting sun should be punished."

"Is that why you walk every night?"

She hesitated a moment before saying, "I want to soak up the whole experience for as long as it lasts. Before you know it, Sean won't need me anymore."

The reminder jolted him even though he'd wanted her work at Cliff House to be done. Maybe because he'd spent so much time trying to forget her beautiful eyes and the smile that transformed her face. He'd also thought a lot about how her full lips would taste followed by self-reproach because she was an employee and he signed her paycheck. Apparently he'd been so preoccupied with all of that, he'd forgotten for a while that her service was temporary. Because Sean *would* recover and wouldn't need her anymore.

She turned to her right, toward the setting sun, and walked into the wind. Her hair blew off her face and he could see the lovely, graceful bone structure. He fell into step beside her and stuck his hands in his pockets as he hunched his shoulders against the cool breeze. They walked in silence for several moments.

Finally she said, "So, I'm guessing you didn't come down here for ocean appreciation day."

"No. I came to see you."

She turned her head to look at him and hair whipped across her face. She tucked it behind her ear. "Is it Sean? Is something wrong?"

"He's fine. It's just you disappeared this afternoon and—"

"When you and Sean were playing on the beach, you mean?"

"Yeah. Was I doing it wrong and you couldn't bear to watch?"

Her mouth pulled tight as sadness crept into her eyes. But when she spoke, her voice snapped with familiar sass and sarcasm. "Oh, please, Gavin. I know you haven't known me that long. But in our short acquaintance have you ever known me to hold back when I had an opinion about something you were doing?"

"No, you definitely call me on my crap." He laughed.

But he remembered their second conversation, when she'd told him she didn't have the heart to work with young children. "You must miss Brian very much."

"I do." She looked down and stepped over a pile of seaweed. "But you and Sean needed time alone together. It wasn't about me."

Something in her tone said it *was* a little about her, but there was no point in pushing it. Whatever was making her pensive was personal and he didn't want to make it his business.

"I just wanted to make sure you're okay."

"Fine." She stuck her hands in the pockets of her sweater. "But why in the world would you think that you were playing wrong? There is no right or wrong. Playing is just—" She shrugged. "Play."

"I didn't have a lot of practice when I was a kid," he admitted.

"That's so sad, Gavin."

"I'm not looking for sympathy." He wasn't sure what he was looking for. Maybe he just needed to say it. "It's just the way it was. I don't think—in fact I'm quite sure my father and I never played."

"What did you do?"

He thought back, trying to recall. Bits and pieces of the past flitted through his mind; things he hadn't considered for a long time. *Don't make so much noise, Gavin.* The housekeeper's voice telling him his father would see him now. Parents' night at school and acting as if he didn't care that no one was there for him.

The memories produced vivid feelings of emptiness and overwhelming loneliness.

Like M.J., he tried to brush it off with humor. "Interactions with my father were more like a report to the board of directors. There was an agenda and we discussed the status of my life."

"You're joking."

"As God is my witness," he denied. "At our quarterly fun fest I got the Spencers' Do Not Fail speech. We excel at every endeavor. My grades were always on the agenda and we discussed them as if they were the rising and falling stock market."

"And did you excel?" she asked.

"Mostly. I got a B once and it wasn't pretty."

"I don't know what to say."

"That's a first."

The real question was why was he saying so much. Maybe a part of him wanted her to understand why he was the way he was.

"Okay. I deserve that." She smiled up at him. "And you're right. I'd have given the old grump a piece of my mind. And I guarantee it wouldn't have been pretty."

"You chewing out my old man?" He laughed. "That would have been something to see." Someone in his corner. A first. "The thing is, weakness and failure weren't tolerated."

"So he's a 'do as I say not as I do' kind of guy?" She looked at him and when he stared cluelessly back, she said, "Hello. He was divorced. Some consider that a failure."

"Ah. I see what you mean. But it would have been a cold day in hell before he'd admit my mother left because the family business was his wife and mistress. He got around the whole failure thing though, by never letting another woman into his life."

"He was a cold, heartless bastard—" She stopped, as if she couldn't believe she'd said that. "No offense."

"None taken." Gavin had often thought the same thing.

"I'm almost afraid to ask. How did he feel about Sean?"

His gut clenched as he recalled his father's first meeting with his infant grandson. Gavin was so proud. This was his child. His flesh and blood. A boy to carry on the family name. He'd never loved anyone the way he loved his son. M.J. was right. His father had been cold and heartless. "He said that because Sean was born outside the bonds of marriage, no good would come of what he called 'the affair.'"

"Oh, Gavin—" She stopped walking and turned to him, her back to the ocean. "Sean is his family, too. And to put that stigma on a perfectly innocent infant is beyond outrageous." She met his gaze. "Is he the reason Sean's mother isn't around?"

His father was the reason Gavin's mother left and never came back. The old man had paid her to go. But the exit of his son's mother was all Gavin's doing—and for good reason. He'd fallen for a beautiful schemer who was only interested in getting her hands on his money.

"Sorry." She held up her hand. "I shouldn't have asked."

And he didn't plan to answer. It was time to

change the subject. She'd grown up without a father and had a husband who'd kept secrets from her. He wanted to know more about that. "Did you grow up in the house where you live now?"

When she nodded, her mouth tightened for a moment. "The Victorian has been in my family for several generations."

"Your mother seems nice."

"She is. But she's also very tough."

"I believe we just established that my father wins that contest hands down."

"Okay. You had to be perfect. I just had to be tidy."

"You want to explain that?" The tide was coming in faster now and he took her hand, tugging her just out of the water's reach.

She slid her fingers from his. "When I was about six, I was left alone with chalk and a blank driveway. In the days before there was such a thing as washable chalk."

"Uh-oh."

"Yeah. But when I got through, I thought that driveway was a masterpiece. My mother had a different opinion."

"Not pretty?"

"My arms still ache when I think about the hours I spent washing it off." She shrugged. "But I learned that I have to be responsible for cleaning up the messes I make. It wasn't about failure. Life is about trial and error and learning."

"Easy to say until a helpless infant is placed in

your arms and is staring up at you. And you're all he's got." When her eyes widened, he said, "What?"

"I guess I didn't see you doing the whole formula and diaper thing."

"I had help, but—" He let out a long breath.

"It wasn't easy, was it?"

"No."

She caught her top lip between her teeth. "I'm sorry I've been so hard on you, Gavin. Sean is a sweet, bright, curious, wonderful child. He didn't get that way by himself."

"Why, Ms. Taylor, you're not going soft on me now, are you?"

"Perish the thought. But when you're not being pushy and arrogant, you have a funny, sensitive side. So some of you has rubbed off on him. And you have good people with him when you can't be."

"Be still my heart," he teased, although he soaked up her words like a dry sponge. The good stuff meant a lot because she didn't hesitate to tell him when he was screwing up.

Her face grew earnest in the silvery moonlight. "The thing is, Gavin, as a teacher I've learned to go the extra mile when I see potential."

"And that pertains to me how?"

"If I call you on your... If I voice my opinion, it's because..." She linked her fingers together as she looked up at him. "The day I first met you, when you tracked me down at school, I met a man who loves his son and wants to be a good father.

Now I see a man who wants to be a better father than his was."

He thought he was, but she made him see that he could be better. "What's the secret?"

"What my aunt Lil said. Yagottawanna. That's what makes you better."

A wave crashed behind her as he stared into her upturned face and the foaming sea rushed toward them. She noticed seconds before it hit her bare feet and jeans. Squealing, she started to scramble past him and, without thinking, he scooped her into his arms.

Her hands clutched his shoulders as she shrieked. Her gaze met his and the laughter disappeared. Her mouth was inches from his own. She was soft and sweet in his arms and her scent invaded his senses— intrusively feminine. Before Gavin knew it, he lowered his mouth to hers.

She tasted of salt air and sunset, sass and spice. Heat pooled in his belly and fired his blood. When he traced the seam of her lips with his tongue, she opened to him and he greedily took what she offered. Suddenly, need throbbed through him and his breathing grew fast and shallow. She was making soft, moaning sounds in her throat while her arms went up and over his shoulders. Her fingers slid into his hair and caressed his neck.

He wanted her here and now, with a yearning as powerful and irresistible as the force of the moon's gravity on the tide.

"Gavin—"

Her breathy whisper, his name on her lips like a caress, the feel of curvy woman in his arms. If he didn't have his hands full, he'd have touched her everywhere. He wanted to feel her skin next to his. He would...

No. He wouldn't. He couldn't.

He pulled his mouth from hers and gulped air into his lungs as if he'd been under water too long. He'd fallen in, all right. But it wasn't a place he could go. Her eyes were heavy-lidded and her mouth moist from his kiss. Her breathing was as ragged as his own. And he wanted her. A hell of a time to realize he should never have kissed her.

Talk about screwing up.

He removed his arm from her legs and let her slide down his front. "That shouldn't have happened. I'm sorry."

Before he could change his mind, he turned and walked back the way they'd come. How could he have done that? He'd felt an odd, vacant sensation when she'd talked about leaving, but that didn't explain the lapse.

The truth wasn't pretty. She wasn't just getting him involved in Sean's therapy. She was *getting* to him.

And he couldn't let that happen.

After her evening walk, M.J. let herself in the front door and quietly shut it behind her. She maintained the nightly ritual, but it wasn't relaxing anymore. Not since Gavin had kissed her a week ago. Now she couldn't stroll along the shore and play tag with the waves and *not* think about that kiss. There were so many things wrong with that, she hardly knew where to start the list.

The feel of his lips on hers was even better than she'd imagined—and she'd imagined it a lot. Then, as suddenly as he'd kissed her, he'd put her down and said he was sorry. That went double for her. Her regret had to do with her elevated pulse, hammering heart and ragged breath. They were the triple storm of proof that she was feeling again. And Gavin was responsible for that.

So now, after her evening exercise, she went to her room and hid. That didn't make her proud, but there was no other word for it.

M.J. was halfway up the stairs when she heard shouting. Her first instinct was to jump in and help, which should have been a giant warning. The fact that she didn't even consider not getting involved should have told her that she was more emotionally invested than was wise.

Instead, she ignored the warning and didn't stop to consider. She raced back downstairs and followed the sound of angry voices to the family room. There she found a father-son standoff. They were facing each other—one tall, dark and handsome, the other small, dark and a heartbreaker-in-training. Both had stubborn and angry written all over them.

Gavin had a hardback children's book in his hand

and she could see that pages had been torn out. They were scattered on the floor.

Sean glared at his father. "Mad."

"Me, too." Gavin glared right back. "We don't destroy books."

The boy shook his head.

"It's not okay, Sean."

He pointed at his father. "Wait."

"Wait?" Gavin shook his head. "For what?"

Sean's little face was fierce with his fury. He picked up one of the pages he'd torn from the book and started to rip it before Gavin took it from him.

"You need to think about this, Sean." He pointed to the doorway. "Go to your room." When the boy stood defiant, he said, "Now."

"Bad," Sean shouted at him, his little body vibrating with anger as he looked at his father. Then he turned and ran from the room.

When he passed her, M.J. could see tears on his cheeks. She wanted to follow him, but first she needed to talk to Gavin.

"What happened?" she asked.

"We were reading. Then he turned into a brat."

There was more to it than that. When Sean acted out, there was usually a trigger, something that frustrated him.

"What set him off?"

Gavin ran his fingers through his hair. "He likes to point to the words and say them."

"Sometimes he can't remember the one he wants."

M.J. moved closer, near enough to feel the heat of him. Near enough to feel the force of the anger still simmering in his eyes.

"I told him the word, but he wouldn't let me turn the page. Then he grabbed the book and started tearing it up."

She understood how hard this was and how much patience it took to deal with this kind of a problem. They were both stubborn; they were both frustrated. But Gavin was the adult.

"Do you remember the first day I came here and we discussed the problems associated with traumatic brain injury?"

"Yes."

She remembered Gavin telling her he wanted his son back the way he was. He needed a reminder of just what he was up against. "The progress is happening, Gavin, but he still struggles with impulse control. He gets frustrated because his language skills were disrupted by the injury. When that happens, he acts out. He wasn't being a brat."

"Could have fooled me," he said.

"You're treating him like a normal child and he isn't. For victims of traumatic brain injury that behavior is normal."

"It's not acceptable for my son," he snapped.

The last time Gavin had observed a meltdown, he'd been impressed with the way she'd handled the situation. This man was being unreasonable. She knew he was angry and reverting to learned behavior.

But her responsibility was to Sean. "Your son is recovering from an accident. For every step forward, there will probably be two steps back. You're the adult. Deal with it."

"I'm dealing with my son as I see fit. He needs to learn self-control. That kind of behavior won't be tolerated in this house."

"Because he's a Spencer?"

"Yes."

She fisted her hands on her hips. "And Spencers aren't permitted failure or weakness?"

Something dark and dangerous glittered in his eyes. "I love my son."

"Yeah. You told me. But are you doing your best to parent him? Are you taking the easy way out? Like your father did?"

"You're on thin ice, lady."

She knew that but couldn't stop herself from saying what had to be said. "I realize you didn't have much of a father figure in your life. But until you make the effort, the pattern won't change."

"What pattern would that be?"

"Expecting perfection. It seems to me that your inclination is to get rid of him instead of showing up for the hard stuff. I can't help wondering if sending Sean to his room is your equivalent of sending him to boarding school."

A muscle contracted in Gavin's jaw as his dark eyes went black with fury. But when he spoke, his voice was calm, like the eye of a hurricane. "You can stop wondering about me because your services are no longer required."

M.J. stared at his stiff back as he walked out. Had he fired her? She sat on the sofa as his words sank in.

Do as I say, not as I do, she thought. For all her preaching about impulse control, she'd gone down the slippery slope without even trying to slow herself down. Now she couldn't be there for Sean. What would happen to him now? She'd established a bond with him and he was responding to therapy. And Gavin...

She knew better; she was a professional. And that was the problem. She hadn't acted like a professional when Gavin had kissed her. And she hadn't acted like a professional just now. Everything had gotten very personal. That wasn't permitted. For her or for him. Now she was out of a job.

That was bad. Even worse was the fact that being unemployed hadn't been her first thought. Her concern had been all about Sean.

And Gavin.

Who was going to call him on his crap? And why did she care so much that it wouldn't be her?

Chapter Nine

"Gavin?"

He turned at the sound of Lenore's voice. The small brunette in her neat navy suit stood in his office doorway.

"What is it?" he asked.

"Sean is wondering where M.J. is."

"Gone."

The expression on his housekeeper's face told him she wanted to say something along the lines of "duh," but she held back. Unlike M.J. who said whatever was on her mind.

Lenore's normally warm brown eyes turned cool. "Sean is actually quite bright. When he didn't see her at breakfast, he noticed right away that she was missing."

Was that sarcasm? This woman's well-bred way of saying "duh?" Gavin leaned against his desk and folded his arms over his chest. Nothing went on in this house that Lenore and her husband didn't know about and he wondered if M.J. had spread rebellion in the ranks during her stay.

Tension knotted inside him. This was his house and he did what was best for everyone in it. Damn, that made him feel as autocratic as his father. But he was trying to do better and just because he'd sent Sean to his room for a time-out didn't mean he was like the old man.

"Gavin?"

He looked up. "Hmm?"

"You need to explain to Sean why M.J. is gone."

"Tell him she was let go."

"He'll ask why."

Did she want to know for Sean or herself? Gavin didn't miss the censure mixed with questions in her eyes.

He fired her because she'd hit a nerve. It was a knee-jerk reaction. But maybe it was for the best. No maybe about it. After kissing her, letting her go was definitely the wisest course of action.

"He doesn't need to know why," Gavin snapped.

"I can't do that to him." Lenore's mouth tightened. "He won't accept it."

"Something's on your mind. Tell me what you really think, Lenore."

The housekeeper nodded. "M.J. is good with Sean. She made a difference in him even a blind man could see. He's not the same boy you brought home from the hospital. He's coming back to us, Gavin."

"You think I was wrong." It wasn't a question.

"I can't say."

M.J. would have said. And then some. She would have told him this was a hill to die on and he needed to show up for the battle.

"Where is Sean?"

"In the family room."

M.J. would have told him he was ignoring his son. Or that he was running away. Or that he was avoiding the hard stuff.

She would have been right.

He nodded. "All right. I'll talk to him."

Gavin found Sean sitting in front of the sofa, half-heartedly walking the dinosaurs up and down his thigh. When he noticed someone in the doorway, his face brightened for a split second before disappointment dulled his eyes.

"Hi, Seanster." Gavin sat on the sofa and the boy leaned against his leg. He brushed his palm over the soft hair that was as dark as his own.

Sean looked up. "M.J.?"

"She had to go away, buddy."

He shook his head. "No."

"I'm sorry."

One question hovered in the solemn dark gaze Sean turned on him. "Why?"

"It was time," was all Gavin could think to say.

Translation: she'd gotten to him. Too close. He'd kissed her. He'd felt something for her and didn't understand it. What he didn't understand he… It was time for her to go away.

"No." Sean lifted his chin, the first sign of stubbornness setting in. "Play."

"Lenore will play with you."

"No. M.J."

How could he explain to his son and make him understand? That M.J. didn't miss a thing and called him on his crap. She didn't let anything slide—not for Sean or him. How could he tell this child he'd kissed her, then lashed out in anger when she'd crossed a line and compared him to his father.

Sean looked up at him. "Miss M.J."

Gavin did, too, but he'd get over it. In a few days he wouldn't miss seeing her smile over coffee. Or the way she did the word jumble in the newspaper before looking at the front page headline. Or her energy when she told Sean it was time for him to work.

"I know you miss her, buddy. But it will be fine."

Sean shook his head. His hands closed into fists around the small plastic animals. Gavin braced himself for the tantrum. M.J. would have encouraged him to use words.

"How do you feel, son?"

"Sad," he said instantly, his little body shaking.

Clearly he'd been coached to get in touch with his emotions.

"Anything else?"

"Mad," he added.

He opened his fists, then grasped the toys and roared sound effects for the dinosaurs as he made them collide, as if they were fighting. At least he hadn't chucked them across the room. That was something. Something M.J. had worked on. Impulse control. Gavin put his hand on the boy's thin shoulder.

"Daddy—" He looked up. "Want M.J. back."

Gavin nodded. "I know you do but—"

"Go see M.J. Now."

"Son, she—" Gavin stared as his heart pounded. Excitement surged through him. "What did you say?"

"M.J. play me. With me," he added.

That was a sentence. This was the first time since before his injury that he'd heard his son stringing words together. Gavin grabbed him up and hugged him.

"Good job, Sean—" His voice cracked.

The little body in his arms squirmed as small hands pushed against his chest. "Daddy—too tight."

"Sorry, buddy. Daddy's just so happy."

He loosened his hold and looked into the face of his child. He didn't realize that he hadn't truly believed Sean would come back to him until this moment. And now...

And now he realized he was the idiot who had fired the person who'd made this miracle happen.

He could find another therapist. She'd said herself

that there were other good ones besides her. But it would take precious time to search and find one. She'd also talked about bonding with a child. That took time, too. And how much time and momentum would Sean lose during the long process? Obviously, Sean had bonded with M.J. What if he wouldn't accept anyone else?

"Daddy—"

Gavin felt little hands on either side of his face as the boy turned it to meet his eager gaze.

"What is it, son?"

"Go see M.J." He touched his own chest. "Me get—me get M.J. back."

There didn't seem to be much choice, Gavin thought grimly. Not if he was going to do what was in his son's best interest.

Gavin nodded. "Okay. We'll go get her back."

There would no doubt be groveling involved.

And money.

But he didn't care how much it cost to convince her to come back. And it wasn't all about Sean. Gavin had started thinking of her differently—as a woman. A woman he wanted. Right now, he couldn't afford to think about how bad that was.

M.J. was trying to convince herself that getting fired was a good thing, but wasn't completely buying the idea. It was late afternoon and she was in her old room, settling back in. The smell of baking wafted up as she sorted through the stack of bills. Since her car was totaled, Henderson had driven her by the house every few days to see her mother and pick up the mail. She didn't get a daily reminder that someone wanted money from her. That was one of the good things about living with Gavin.

The kiss had been pretty good, too, but she wasn't going to think about that.

First thing that morning she'd notified the school district that she was available to substitute for summer school. She would borrow her mother's car until she could figure out transportation. Then she paid bills and took inventory. She'd negotiated more time for the balloon payment, but right now she had no income at all. If by some miracle she subbed every day, there still wouldn't be enough money. She was going to miss one job for the pay of two.

She'd only been responsible for Sean's therapy, which had given her plenty of time to tell Gavin what she thought about his parenting style.

And that's what had gotten her fired.

At least his stubborn arrogance and pigheaded parenting style were out there, no secret. Unlike her husband who'd hidden his gambling problem while he was bringing down the foundation of her world. But that was her mess and she would clean it up. However long it took, she thought, carefully putting the stack of invoices and receipts into the expandable folder and tucking it into her bottom drawer. Now she had a car mess to work out, too.

Glancing around her room at the pink bedspread

and bay window, she realized she'd missed it. And her family. So maybe getting fired was a good thing. Although now she missed Sean. And Gavin. Her feelings were veering into messy and complicated. She'd gotten out with just minor cuts and bruises on her heart. But last night sleep had been a long time coming as she'd thought about Sean, how he would wonder why she wasn't there, why she hadn't said goodbye.

And the warmth of Gavin's mouth teasing her own.

She'd forget about it. She'd go downstairs and help with dinner—and put on a happy face so they didn't know she was hurting inside. That would take her mind off things. As she descended, the mouth-watering aroma of Aunt Lil's chocolate chip cookies drifted to her.

"Home sweet home," she said.

When she walked into the kitchen her aunt was just taking a pan of cookies out of the oven.

"Hello, dear," she said.

"Can I have one?" M.J. tested one of them with a finger to see if it was cool enough.

"Someone has to sacrifice their hips to see if these suckers are any good."

"I live to serve."

M.J. took one cooling on the rack. If you caught it just right, the cookie would be warm and soft, the chocolate chip part gooey and rich—and you wouldn't burn the roof of your mouth. Timing was everything when one was using sugar to forget a handsome millionaire. She bit into the cookie and savored the flavors that all mixed together and became the world's best.

She sighed. "Aunt Lil, I could become a serious comfort-eater. One bite and all the problems are gone. There's just me and chocolate."

Her mother walked in the back door with an armful of yellow roses. "She's right, Lil. You should market these and give Famous Amos some serious competition in the dog-eat-dog cookie world."

Her sister laughed. "I'd have to come up with a clever name. Famous Lil just doesn't have the same ring."

M.J. chewed the last bite as she thought. "Lil's luscious little… Can either of you think of an L-word for cookie?"

Evelyn pulled great-grandmother Anna's crystal vase from the cupboard above the refrigerator, then set it on the counter beside the sink. She looked at M.J. over her shoulder. "I can think of another L-word. Four letters. Ends in E. And there could be one hot millionaire attached to it."

Had M.J. somehow betrayed her feelings? Was it a mom thing and she somehow *knew* Gavin had kissed her? M.J. looked at her aunt and determined more comfort eating was called for. "Can I have another cookie?"

"Of course. But you can eat the whole batch and it won't make you feel any better. Your mother's right. Want to talk about it?"

M.J. looked from her aunt's kindly expression to her mother's concerned and curious one, and sighed. "The downside of living with women is a weight problem and nowhere to hide emotionally."

Evelyn looked calm as she trimmed the rose stems with hand clippers, then placed them in the vase. But when she glanced over her shoulder, the expression in her blue eyes said she could just as easily cut out the offending man's heart with the garden tool.

"What happened with Gavin?"

Besides that kiss? For a split second M.J. was afraid she'd said that out loud. No point in going there. She didn't work for him anymore. End of problem. She should be grateful. And she would. As soon as she could manage to stop missing his big-bad-wolf smile and the quick-witted conversation. She took another cookie. Cookie therapy was the only way to go.

"I told you, Mom. He fired me."

"That's ridiculous," her mother snorted. "You're a good therapist."

"I do my best."

There must have been something in her voice, because her mother looked up sharply. "Did he have a reason? Or was he just being stupid?"

"He had a reason because I told him he was being stupid. So I guess you could say both."

Aunt Lil shook her head. "There's nothing more dangerous than a man who can't take constructive criticism."

"I suppose I deserved it," M.J. said. "There was a situation with Sean and I thought Gavin could have handled it better. Sometimes parents of TBI kids need help dealing with the situation, too."

"And you told him," Aunt Lil said, waving her spatula like a symphony conductor. "Good for you."

Not so good, M.J. thought. Something inside her hurt and she wasn't sure if it was too many cookies or missing the Spencer men.

"It's too bad," her mother said. "You're really a talented therapist." She sighed as their gazes met. "I was happy to see you doing it again. It was hard seeing you pull away from what you love since losing Brian."

Even as her heart squeezed tight, M.J. saw the sympathy in her mother's expression and knew she missed her grandson, too. "It hurt so much after I lost him. And it hurt working with Sean at first. But eventually I found that I'd really missed children. The energy. The laughter. The innocent sweetness."

But it was the father who'd tapped into her senses and made her feel dangerous feelings, things better not felt.

Evelyn smiled. "I'm glad to hear that, sweetie. In spite of the way it ended, at least something good came out of the experience."

"I suppose that's one way to look at it," M.J. said. Absently she picked up another cookie and munched on it.

The doorbell rang and the three of them looked at each other.

"Are either of you expecting anyone?" M.J. asked.

"No," Aunt Lil said. "And it's not like this is a regular neighborhood where schoolkids show up selling candy bars for a fund-raiser."

"I'll go," M.J. said.

She had no idea who it was, but it had to be about her, and probably that wasn't good. She lifted the lace curtain on the window beside the door. This was definitely about her. Gavin stood there. With Sean. It was a one-two punch. The father made her heart pound. The son melted it.

Taking a deep breath, she opened the door. Before she could say anything, Sean grinned his big-bad-wolf-in-training grin. "M.J."

He threw himself against her and she went down on one knee and took him in her arms. "Hi, kiddo."

He squeezed her tight, then stepped back. "Daddy took me work. Today."

Her eyes widened as she stared at the little boy. Then she stood and met Gavin's gaze. "A sentence?"

He nodded. "This morning. It took me a couple beats to realize it."

His way of giving her a compliment for getting it right away? She bent and gave Sean another hug. "Good job, Sean." She stepped back and held up her hand. "High five, kiddo."

The child slapped her palm, then suddenly looked shy as he stared past her at the two women behind M.J. in the doorway.

"Sean Spencer, this is my family." She held out her

hand indicating each of them in turn. "My mother and Aunt Lil."

"Hello again, Gavin," her aunt said, her gaze narrowing. Fortunately the spatula wasn't in her hand when she held it out to shake his. "I just made cookies. If I'd known you were coming, I'd have made a special one just for you."

He looked uncomfortable. "Nice to see you again."

Yeah, M.J. thought. And if he was smart, he wouldn't be eating or drinking anything at their house.

M.J. met his gaze. "I'm happy for you, Gavin. And Sean. It was good of you to bring him over. I didn't get a chance to say goodbye."

"About that," he started, running his hand through his hair. "I'd like to talk to you for a moment."

The older women exchanged a look, then her mother spoke up. "Sean," she said, bending down to his level, "would you like a cookie?"

"Yes," the little boy said eagerly, putting his hand into hers.

"Chocolate chip?" Gavin asked.

M.J. nodded. "How did you know?"

He brought his knuckle to the corner of her mouth and brushed something away. "Evidence."

And that was the worst possible moment for everyone to leave them alone.

"Why did you take Sean to work?" she asked.

Gavin stuck his hands in the pockets of his dark brown slacks. His tie was loose and the pale yellow sleeves of his shirt were rolled up. "He had a major breakthrough. I couldn't leave him."

Wow. Sean wasn't the only one who'd had a major breakthrough. "That's good, Gavin."

His gaze turned intense. "The thing is, work is going to get nuts."

"Oh?"

"R & D just finished new productivity software and the launch is imminent. I'll be heavily involved in marketing. Looking for a new speech therapist will be time-consuming. So, I'd be willing to take you back."

"Willing?" She stared at him for several moments, then laughed. "You give new meaning to the word *arrogant*."

"Don't you think it's important to strike while the iron is hot? To build on this breakthrough?"

"Absolutely."

"Good, then I'll expect you—"

"Wait a second. I didn't agree to anything."

He sighed. "Of course you didn't. That would have been too easy. And completely out of character for you."

She shut the front door. "I'm trying to decide whether or not you just insulted me."

"That wouldn't be an especially smart negotiating technique on my part since I'm trying to hire you back."

"I'm no less outspoken today than I was last night when you fired me for it. Why should we go through that again?"

He met her gaze. "You were right about everything you said."

"Conversely, that would mean you were wrong," she pointed out.

He lifted a shoulder. "I'll admit I could have handled the situation better."

"How do I know we wouldn't go through the same thing again?"

"You don't. I don't," he said honestly. "I can only promise that I'll do the best I know how to be a father to my son. I'll listen to what you have to say and try to do what you ask."

She couldn't ask him to make her feelings for him go away. And right now she was liking him a whole lot more. He wasn't a man who would come right out and say he was wrong—that would be admitting failure and he'd been trained not to do that. But he'd certainly flirted with the W-word in his apology. He hadn't promised not to get frustrated in dealing with difficult parenting problems, either, but she couldn't ask that. It went with the territory under ordinary circumstances, and a child like Sean wasn't ordinary. Gavin had promised what he could deliver—his best. No one could ask more than that.

And Sean was such a sweetheart. She wanted to continue working with him, to teach him as much as she could. The truth was, he'd taught her something, too. He'd broken down her barriers and shown her how much she'd missed being with children.

The problem now was Gavin and her attraction

to him. It would be stupid to pretend it didn't exist. Not after that kiss. And she couldn't begin to understand why he'd done it, because she so wasn't his type. That made going back tantamount to asking for trouble. After attraction came need. Needing a man, counting on him, wasn't something she would do again.

She was about to tell him that when the front door burst open and Sean came running out. He looked up at her, his eyes shining, his freckle-splashed nose impossibly cute. "M.J. come back my house. Now."

She ruffled his hair. "About that, kiddo—"

"I won't throw toys," he said earnestly. "I be good."

"Me, too," Gavin promised.

If his look was just earnest, there would have been no question. But it was intense, and sexy, and charismatic.

When she didn't say anything, Gavin took a step forward and settled his big hand on Sean's shoulder. "Sean needs you. He's the most important person in my life. Therefore I need you. If you want me to grovel, I will."

"It's not about that, Gavin."

"Okay." His eyes grew dark. "I'll make it worth your while. What will it take? Name your price."

She'd have said her price was him not messing with her heart, but his words convinced her that wouldn't be a problem. His issues would make him keep his distance. As long as he believed money was her motivation, she was safe from him.

"All right, Gavin. I'll come back. At the same salary. It's more than generous."

Chapter Ten

M.J. stood over the two Spencer men playing in the sand at the water's edge. "What are you building?"

"M.J." Sean grinned. "Me and Daddy—digging."

"I see that," she answered, making a mental note to work on that speech pattern.

She'd been back a week and it seemed as if the child was making milestone-type progress every day. She wondered if it had anything to do with the fact that his father was spending more time with him. Every day, Gavin was home from work while it was still light enough to play outside. This in spite of his claim that he'd be too busy to spare time for a therapist search.

He'd been right. The interruption in therapy would

have slowed Sean's progress. Apparently Gavin *was* capable of listening and learning.

"Building castle," Sean said proudly.

M.J. glanced at the unrecognizable pile of dark brown sand. "Nice job. You guys look thirsty."

"I guess we look that way because we are." Gavin brushed the back of one hand across his forehead.

She set down the small cooler beside them. "Lenore thought you might like something to drink. I volunteered to bring it. I have juice boxes and soda."

"No beer?" Gavin straightened, then sat back on his heels.

"Sorry." She angled her thumb toward the wooden stairs she'd just come down. "I can go back and get one."

"Don't bother. Soda's fine."

"How about you, Seanster? Want some juice?" she asked, sliding the cooler lid sideways. She pulled out a can and handed it to Gavin. Their fingers brushed and even the ice-cold aluminum didn't stop the burst of heat.

Sean nodded eagerly. "Apple."

She bent and retrieved it. Anything to break eye contact with Gavin.

When Sean held out a sandy hand, she shook her head. "Just a sec." She took off the plastic, then put the straw in the tiny hole. "Here you go."

"Thank you," he said politely.

Gavin glanced at the boy, then slid her a wry look. "That's humbling."

"What?"

"My manners have been upstaged by a six-year-old." He lifted the soda can. "Thank you."

"You're both welcome." She closed the cooler lid.

"Aren't you having one?"

She shook her head. "I have to get back."

"Because?"

"I have to…"

"What?" Gavin popped the tab on the soda. "A date? Big plans to organize your sock drawer? Matters of national security?"

"All of the above," she said, laughing.

"Makes me tired just thinking about it. You probably need a break. Stick around."

Sean dropped his plastic shovel and jumped up, then put his gritty hand in hers. "Stay, M.J. Me—" He thought for a moment. "*With* me and Daddy."

The now familiar melting sensation trickled through her and she tapped his nose as she smiled into the sweet, eager face. "How can I refuse an offer like that from such a handsome gentleman? Socks and national security will just have to wait."

"Okay." The boy nodded.

"Okay," she agreed.

"Need cement, Daddy." Sean picked up his bucket and raced toward the ocean, his drink forgotten.

"Cement?"

Gavin rubbed his nose as he sat and watched his son. "Water. Mix it with sand."

"And you get?"

"Sandy water," Gavin said. "But if you use your imagination, it's cement, the glue that holds the castle together."

"I see."

He took a long swallow of soda and M.J. was fascinated by the purely male sight of his Adam's apple moving. The muscles in his strong neck worked as he drained the contents of the can. It was a completely innocent movement, but highlighted her conflict. Gavin possessed an underlying shimmer of raw sexuality that stirred something inside her every time she was in the same room with him. Technically, the beach was a wide-open space. But apparently it wasn't wide enough, nor was there sufficient space to take the edge off her reaction.

He looked up at her and closed one eye against the glare of the sun getting lower in the sky. "I'm taking five. Why don't you take a load off?" he asked, patting the sand beside him.

Not a good idea, she thought. "Maybe I should help Sean bring in more cement."

"You could." Gavin glanced at the boy, kneeling at the water's edge, playing. "But there's a problem."

"What?"

"One bucket. Bringing water back and forth in your hands—" He shook his head. "Not efficient."

"I see your point." And she was left with two choices—sit or run away and look stupid. She sat.

She watched the child jumping in the water as each gentle wave rolled onto the sand. She stared at the expanse of blue ocean and the cloudless sky above. She glanced to her right, noting the jagged cliffs and the small rock formations. Anything to keep from looking at Gavin as the silence grew between them.

"Nice day," he said.

When silence gets awkward, you can't go wrong talking about the weather, she thought. "Yes. Really nice."

"Not too windy. Not too warm." He rested his wrist on one upraised knee. His shorts were wet. "Just right."

"How's the water?"

"Not too cold, not too warm—"

"Just right?" she asked, her mouth curving up.

"Yeah. This is like a bad imitation of *Goldilocks and the Three Bears*." He met her gaze. "It seems when you're not yelling at me, you have nothing to say."

"I don't recall raising my voice. And I have lots to say."

"Care to share?"

"For starters, since I've been rehired, you've been home early every day. That seems unusual for a man who is preparing a product launch."

"About that," he said sheepishly. "I stretched the truth some."

"Oh?"

"R & D is finished with the software. But the launch isn't as imminent as I implied. I was using everything I could think of to convince you to come back to work."

"Really?" She put as much innocent sarcasm as possible into her tone. "And yet you were merely *willing* to take me back."

He rubbed a finger beneath his nose. "Here's the thing about arrogance you may not know. It's a facade."

"You're right. I didn't know."

He looked at her. "I expected it to be harder to convince you to work for me again."

"I know what you're thinking," she said.

"Ah," he said, staring at his son. "A mind reader. I'm impressed. So what am I thinking?"

"It wasn't the money," she assured him. Then she shrugged. "Well, maybe a little. A girl has to make a living."

"Yes, she does." His expression was unreadable.

"It's just that I realized you were right."

"There's a first." Surprise flickered across the lean planes of his face. "Words I never thought I'd hear from you. What was I right about?"

She trailed a finger through the fine white sand. "It was the second time I saw you—"

"Apparently I'm right so infrequently you can recall the exact time."

She laughed. "It's not that. I remember because you came to the house. You were trying to convince me to work with Sean and I was resisting."

"Okay." He stared at her expectantly. "I'm waiting for you to get to the part where I was right."

"You said that losing my son should motivate me to help other children."

"M.J., I—" He shook his head. "I didn't mean to hurt you. It was desperation talking."

"I know that now." Without thinking, she put her hand on his arm. It was warm and strong and sent sparks arcing through her. "Don't you want to hear the good part?"

"Okay."

"If I could change what happened to my child, I'd do it in a heartbeat. But I can't. The only way to make sense of something senseless is to find some meaning."

"What did you find?" he asked, his tone gentle.

"I found it in Sean. He taught me that I missed being around kids. And—"

"What?" The empty can dangled from his fingers as he rested his forearm on his knee.

"Instead of mourning my son's loss, I needed to celebrate his spirit by helping children."

Staring at Sean rolling in the sand, he swallowed hard. "The difference you made in my son is incredible. I can't tell you how grateful I am."

"The difference he made in me is remarkable, too."

Their gazes locked and understanding surged between them. And something else that put a hitch in her breathing. Their shoulders brushed; their faces were inches apart. Gavin barely moved, but she felt him bend toward her. A shout from Sean broke the spell.

"Daddy. M.J. Look," he said, walking stiffly toward them. He stopped a foot away and the image wasn't pretty. Sand stuck to him everywhere he was wet.

"You're a mess, Seanster," Gavin said, groaning.

M.J. shook her head. "You look like someone dipped you in sugar. Just like one of my aunt Lil's sugar cookies."

The boy laughed. "I like cookies. Me want—" He stopped. "I want to—"

"What, sweetie?" she asked.

"Go your—go *to* your house again."

"For cookies?" she asked. "I don't know. I haven't worked out my car situation since the accident—"

"I can put a car and driver at your disposal," Gavin offered.

Of course he could. Because he was a millionaire.

For a little while M.J. had forgotten that, because being a millionaire didn't define him. She'd been drawn to the father, a flawed man trying his best for his son. She'd also been drawn to the man who had opened up to her, then kissed her breathless not too far from where they were sitting right now. And she'd sworn he was about to do it again before Sean interrupted them.

"Please, M.J.," Sean pleaded. "Go to your house."

She looked at Gavin. "If you're sure you don't mind."

"Not a problem."

"Okay, then. Thanks."

For the reminder, too, that he had a lot of money and questioned motivations because of it. Gavin would always be wealthy and wary and she would be lucky to dig her way out of debt in this lifetime.

The differences would always stand between them and she couldn't afford to forget it.

* * *

"Gavin." M.J. stood in the open doorway of her house. "I was expecting Henderson to pick us up."

"I was on my way home from work anyway. It's no problem to do chauffeur duty."

Gavin had known the two of them were going to visit her family and had called Cliff House to see if they were back yet. M.J. had noticed that lately he structured his workday to spend as much time as possible with Sean. His office staff was getting the message that he was out of there—unless someone was bleeding or on fire.

"Come in." M.J. opened the door wider and stood back to allow him inside. "I'll get Sean. He's in the back, gardening with my mother. She loves her roses. And he seems to like helping her, but I think it has more to do with a legitimate excuse to get dirty."

"I guess just being a boy isn't enough."

She laughed. "I guess not."

Gavin noted the pink color in her cheeks. "Speaking of roses... There's a healthy color in your face these days."

The blush highlighted her perfect skin and made her eyes seem bigger, bluer. Her hair, straight and sun-streaked, fell around her face like golden silk. It was disconcerting that he no longer thought of her as pale and plain. There was something so appealingly innocent about her.

"What do you know? Color that's not from a

healing bruise." Self-consciously she touched her cheek, just below her eye. "I guess Cliff House agrees with me."

And there it was. The remark struck a chord and reminded him that she could have an agenda beyond Sean's therapy. Obviously she was worth what he was paying her. She was bringing his son back to him. But if M. J. Taylor had any plans about something more with Gavin, something long-term, legal and permanent, she was in for a reality check. A woman had used him once to get a lot of money. *His* agenda didn't include being that stupid or gullible again. No matter how innocent she seemed, he couldn't take the chance and risk another failure.

He looked around the living room. "This is very different from Cliff House."

It was the first time he'd been here and not been preoccupied with trying to hire her as a speech therapist. The furnishings were not contemporary. Dark wood tables book-ended a green-and-gold brocade sofa with curved arms and a high back. The grouping sat on a floral area rug in the center of the wooden floor. A mahogany dining room table with eight chairs and a matching buffet were tucked into the corner beneath a crystal chandelier. Framed photos were everywhere, some very old black-and-white ones, some more recent in color. They covered tables and hung on the walls.

Gavin looked down at her. "This is like stepping into another era."

"I know. It's an antique lover's fantasy. There's china, glassware, pictures and furniture from my great-grandparents' day. They built the house and every generation since has grown up here."

Pride shone in her eyes as she glanced around the room. "I love this place."

She looked sincere, but he couldn't help wondering if it agreed with her as much as Cliff House. And he realized that he wanted to be wrong about her having an agenda.

"So, besides stopping to smell the roses, what has my son been up to?" he asked. Sean was a safe topic.

"He's been helping Aunt Lil bake cookies."

He sniffed. "I thought I smelled something good."

"There's one in the kitchen with your name on it," she said, smiling.

"Twist my arm."

He followed her through the house, his gaze dropping to her curvy little butt. Worn denim hugged her hips and thighs. Her short legs didn't go on forever, but they looked good, too good—and they were definitely long enough to wrap around his waist when making love.

Jeez. The worst part was that the thought didn't surprise him. It didn't come out of nowhere. He'd been thinking about sex and M.J. ever since the night he'd kissed her. He'd almost made the same mistake a few days ago, this time in broad daylight, with his son playing a few feet away in the sand. How could he not trust her and still want her to the point of distraction? She was a weakness he wouldn't indulge. No one knew better than he did that women used sex as a weapon.

They walked into the kitchen where M.J.'s apron-clad aunt was just taking a pan out of the oven. After setting it on a rack beside the stove, she looked at him and smiled. "Hello, Gavin."

"Ms. Taylor."

"Oh, please. Call me Lil."

"Lil it is."

The last time he'd seen her, her hostility had been as hot as the fresh-baked cookies. Lil had made some not-so-veiled threats about poisoning him for firing her niece. He was pretty sure she'd been kidding, and knew it was about her family circling the wagons to protect their own, and wondered how unconditional support like that felt. He wouldn't know since his father hadn't been into the touchy-feely stuff. What an odd pair he and M.J. were. She'd never known her father and he barely remembered his mother.

They were like two halves of the same coin. And the thought disturbed him.

Just then the back door opened and Evelyn came inside with a sniffling Sean.

"What's wrong?" Gavin asked, instantly concerned.

"A thorny situation." Evelyn shrugged at the pun. "Nothing serious."

"Daddy." Sean ran over to him and held up his dirty hand. "Hurt myself."

Gavin went down on one knee and studied the

puncture wound and trickle of blood on the little thumb. "I see, Seanster. It doesn't look too bad."

"I'll get something to clean it up," M.J. volunteered, then left the room.

"We'll fix that right up. Did you have fun, Sean?" Gavin asked to distract him.

The boy nodded enthusiastically and his face brightened. "Made cookies. I cut roses."

"We need to get you some gloves that fit those little hands so you don't get stuck next time." Evelyn smiled. "Would you like that?"

"Yes."

Sean seemed very comfortable here, Gavin thought. He looked at the older women and wondered, not for the first time, if Sean missed the maternal touch. He had Henderson and Lenore. They were kind and caring, and they loved the boy, but it was different somehow. In this house, you could almost reach out and hold the warmth in the palm of your hand.

M.J. hurried back into the room with cotton balls, a brown bottle of hydrogen peroxide, a tube of ointment and a couple of Band-Aids. She set the items on the counter by the sink and moved a chair over.

"Okay, kiddo, hop up here and let's have a look at that thumb."

Sean climbed up, but looked doubtful as he held his hand behind his back. "Will it hurt?"

"Maybe a little. But if we don't clean it, your thumb could get infected and that would hurt more." M.J.'s expression was thoughtful as she picked up the bottle. "This looks like water, but it will make bubbles."

"Really?" Sean was intrigued.

"It foams up and gets the dirt out," M.J. promised.

Lil moved to his other side. "When your thumb is all clean, you can have a cookie."

Evelyn stood behind the chair. "Two cookies. One for each hand. And you can take some home."

"Okay." Sean extended his arm over the sink and stuck out his thumb.

Circling the wagons for one of their own, Gavin thought, looking at the women surrounding his son. And he wasn't entirely sure how he felt about it.

When first aid was successfully completed, they sat at the kitchen table and had cookies all around, with milk for Sean and coffee for the adults. Gavin glanced at the clock and was surprised to see he'd been here over an hour. Reluctantly, he said it was time for them to go home.

"Don't want to go." The child's mouth pulled into a stubborn line.

"Dinner's waiting," Gavin said.

"I want to eat at M.J.'s house."

Gavin sighed. The good news was his son had strung a lot of words into a long sentence. The bad news: it was a long sentence declaring rebellion in the ranks.

M.J. stood, then bent down to Sean's level. When he swung his legs back and forth, she wrapped her fingers around his calf. "Sean, do you want to come visit again?" When he nodded, she smiled. "Good.

Me, too. So, how about this? Next time you can stay for dinner."

"Daddy, too?"

She met his gaze and the pulse in her neck fluttered. "Daddy, too." She looked at Sean. "What's your favorite dinner? Wait," she said when he started to answer. "Let me guess. Hot dogs?"

"With mus—mustard. And fries. French," he added, as if that was very important.

"Next time we'll plan ahead for dinner."

"Okay," Sean said, hopping off the chair. "Let's go, Daddy."

And just like that a crisis was averted. She made it look easy, but there was nothing simple about this. There was no question that M.J. was good at what she did. But Gavin wasn't sure if she was also manipulating her situation to milk it for all it was worth. What worried him the most was that Sean might be getting too attached to her. Was she encouraging it? Trying to use his child to get to him?

It wouldn't be the first time.

Everyone walked to the front door to see them out. As M.J. gathered her purse from the table in the entry, Sean stood beside her, studying the framed photos.

"Who's that?" he asked, pointing to a woman with a beautiful blond little girl on her lap.

"That's me," M.J. answered. "That's my mom."

Sean stared at the picture for several moments, then turned to Gavin with a serious expression on his face. "Daddy? Where's my mommy?"

Chapter Eleven

M.J. hadn't said anything when Gavin danced around his son's question. And she didn't say anything through dinner. Now Sean was in bed asleep and she and Gavin were sitting outside on the wooden deck overlooking the Pacific. It was a beautiful evening and he'd brought two glasses and a bottle of wine. They sat side-by-side on the cushioned swing, gently rocking back and forth.

"You have to talk to Sean about his mother, Gavin."

"Why?"

"Because he asked." M.J. sipped her wine and let the cold, bold taste linger on her tongue. "It's about trust. If you don't tell him something about the hard stuff, you lose credibility on everything else. Or…"

He glanced sideways. "What?"

"He'll come to his own conclusions and they'll be wrong." She let out a long breath.

"What wrong conclusions did you live with?" His voice was surprisingly gentle given the tension in it a moment before.

"How did you know?"

"Educated guess. Your father wasn't around. I picked up on it because I'm a sensitive guy." He shrugged, his shoulder brushing hers. "I don't know."

"Well, Mr. Sensitive, you're right. I was about Sean's age when I overheard my mother tell Aunt Lil that my father was selfish and self-centered. That he'd left for someone better."

"Obviously that was his problem."

"I know that now, as a rational adult. But six-year-old sensibility believed it was all about me. The message was that if I wasn't a very good girl, my family would leave and I'd be alone."

He sucked in a deep breath, then let it out. "And you never said anything to your mother?"

"I was supposed to be in bed, but I'd sneaked downstairs and was listening. I was already being bad. I was afraid if I said anything I'd lose everyone I loved. So I just tried to be the best little girl in the world."

Gavin thought about that. "Okay. So he walked out on his family. How do you tell a kid that?"

"First you let the child know it's not about them. Then spin the truth into something less painful. You say he wasn't happy. That he needed something you couldn't give." She shrugged.

"There's no way to spin what Sean's mother did," he snapped, his voice as hard and sharp as the cliffs below them. "And I gave her exactly what she wanted."

Quiet surrounded them except for the rhythmic sound of the surf. Strategically placed spotlights illuminated the yard. A nearly full moon dripped silver around them. If circumstances were different, if they were different people, the setting would be rampant with romance. But they were who they were.

The savage anger and loathing in Gavin's voice was frightening. As their shoulders brushed, she could feel his tension and the hostility that radiated from him. Whatever happened, it was about money. He'd already told her that. And she knew he distrusted her and suspected she manipulated him to get as much as she could for doing his son's speech therapy. If he knew the extent of her financial trouble, it would leave no doubt in his mind that she was as bad as Sean's mother. But how bad was she?

M.J. shifted and tucked her legs up, angling her knees toward his thigh. Gavin sat stiff and stoic, feet on the ground, still swinging them. After draining the contents of his glass, he set it on the table beside them, next to the bottle.

She wanted to help, but that couldn't happen without knowing the facts. It was likely he'd clam up. Still she had to try. For Sean's sake.

"What did you give her, Gavin? What was it she wanted?"

"What else?" He laughed, a bitter, ugly sound that poisoned the beauty of the night. "Money."

"How did she get it? Blackmail? Fraud?" She remembered her mother saying there were newspaper stories about the bachelor millionaire. "Did she threaten to go to the media?"

A muscle in his lean cheek contracted. "I suppose what she did encompassed all of the above in a way." He met her gaze. "And the worst part was that my father warned me."

She didn't need to ask the nature of the warning. If a child grows up with cynicism, he learns to be a cynic. Gavin had been conditioned to believe that everyone had their price. It shamed her that she proved the rule and not the exception.

"But the moment I saw Avery, advice, caution and common sense went out the window. Go ahead and say it." The look he turned on her was intense although his tone held a hint of irony.

A beautiful name for a beautiful woman. Although she couldn't help thinking it was awfully close to avarice.

"Say what?"

"That I was thinking with my other, smaller brain."

"Pardon the pun, but that would be a low blow." Her cheeks heated. Fortunately in the dim light he wouldn't be able to see.

He smiled at her words, but the humor didn't

spread to his dark eyes. There was only betrayal and bitterness. "The point is, she's the most beautiful woman I'd ever seen. One look and I didn't believe anything my father had said. Someone who looked like an angel couldn't be just about money."

It sounded a lot like love, she thought, her heart twisting almost to the point of pain. "What happened?"

"She chased me until I caught her."

"Played hard to get?"

"Played me for a fool, is more accurate. She baited the hook, then reeled me in. And made me love every minute." He rubbed his hands over his face. "Then she informed me she was pregnant."

M.J. went cold as what he was saying slowly pieced itself together. "In this day and age there's very little reason for an unplanned pregnancy."

"She'd told me she was on the pill, and a course of antibiotics blocked the effects."

"But you didn't believe her."

"Not a chance."

"Why?"

"I was thrilled about becoming a father and asked her to marry me."

The pain in her chest pulled a little tighter. "What did she say?"

Again he laughed and it was tainted with sarcasm. He shook his head, the picture of self-contempt. "The words 'romantic fool' come to mind."

He'd told her he loved her, M.J. realized. He'd fallen in love with the woman who was using her assets to manipulate and defraud. "What about the pregnancy?"

"Once I revealed that I was all in favor of the baby, she got to her real agenda. She said if I paid her enough money she wouldn't terminate the pregnancy."

"Oh, my God—" She felt the need to touch him and put her hand on his arm, feeling him tense. The shock of his words sank in slowly. This was so far beyond what she'd imagined. The sheer deviousness of the scheme boggled the mind. How callous and unconscionable.

Anger shimmered in the gaze he settled on her. "What kind of woman holds a child's life hostage?"

"What kind of man doesn't call her bluff?"

"That's just it. She wasn't bluffing. She would have terminated the life of my child without hesitation. I couldn't let that happen."

"So you paid her off."

"After getting proof, yes." He nodded. "I bought her a luxury condo, found the best obstetrician. Went to every doctor's appointment. And was with her when Sean was born. But there's one thing I hadn't expected."

"What?"

"Sean Carson Spencer—my son. When I held that little boy in my arms for the first time, I hadn't counted on how much love I could feel for such a small scrap of humanity."

This was the man who refused to let an unprincipled witch terminate the pregnancy. This was the man who could break a woman's heart. Emotion pulled tight in M.J.'s chest and moisture blurred her eyes. But when she blinked away the tears, the look on his face told her there was more.

"What, Gavin?"

"From the moment I first held him, I made up my mind to give my son the best. Money had bought him, but I decided to take it a step farther."

"How?"

"I gave her a bonus if she signed off any rights to him. I bought him a future without his scheming, gold-digging mother in it. She took the money and ran."

More than that, M.J. realized. She took his heart and stomped on it. Gavin was left with a child to raise on his own and a father who never let him forget his failure to realize that everyone has a price.

"I see," she said, blowing out a long breath. "And I don't quite know what to say."

"How uncharacteristic of you." For the first time his smile wasn't tinged with tension.

She shook her head. "The best I can come up with is what I said before. Make sure he knows her absence isn't about him. And that's the honest truth. The rest of what I said could work, too. His mother isn't happy and never will be. She has no con-science and is looking for something no one can give her."

"So I should lie and tell Sean she loves him?"

"Normally I wouldn't condone deceit, but you

can't tell him the truth." She blew out a long breath. "You're right about one thing."

"I like being right."

"Not this time. There's no way to spin what happened into something a six-year-old child can understand. I'm a grown-up and I don't understand it."

But something he'd said came through loud and clear. He'd fallen in love with a calculating, conniving, underhanded woman and been used in an unthinkable way. Children learn what they live. Gavin's father had taught him by example that when you fail at love don't try again. If he followed that example, he would never let himself care again.

Any woman who let herself care for him was sure to be at the very least disappointed. At most? Destroyed.

Gavin walked into the house through the door connecting to the garage and stopped in his office, dropping his briefcase by his desk. He picked up the stack of mail and looked through it.

"I thought I heard the garage." M.J. stood in the doorway, curvy and feminine in jeans and a pink T-shirt. "Hi."

Her soft voice reached inside him and yanked on his nerve endings, snapping them to attention. "Hi. I guess Sean's in bed?"

She nodded. "But not that long ago. He might still be awake."

"I'll go see."

"Henderson and Lenore left for the night."

"I know. I told them not to wait for me since you're here with Sean." His gaze was drawn to her chest when she folded her arms.

"If you're hungry, I could fix you something to eat."

"There wasn't time for dinner. I am hungry." And not just for food, he thought, looking at the full curve of her lower lip.

His body stirred with desire. Something that didn't happen when the other members of the house staff greeted him in the evening. In fact, this was the first time in a long time someone besides paid staffers had met him.

"I'll warm up tonight's lasagna and throw together a salad."

"Sounds good. Don't go to a lot of trouble."

"No trouble for the boss." She smiled, then backed out of the doorway and disappeared.

He stared at the empty space where she'd stood a moment ago. She *was* a paid staffer. When had he stopped thinking of her that way?

The day on the beach when he'd almost kissed her?

Maybe it was the afternoon he'd watched her clean and bandage Sean's scratch. Or talking with her about his son's mother and brainstorming strategies to answer his question about her. He'd never talked to anyone about how Sean had been conceived. Not even his father—especially not his father.

He probably wouldn't have said anything to M.J. if she hadn't heard Sean ask the question. In a perfect world, the boy would have a father and a mother, but this wasn't a perfect world. It was never too early to learn that. Gavin was getting daily lessons when he faced M.J. and struggled with not crossing the line with her.

He wasn't sure when the shift happened, but she'd become a staple at Cliff House—like coffee and milk. Even more disturbing was the realization that a part of him expected to see her and was looking forward to it. He was afraid he'd hear the words, "Honey, I'm home," come out of his mouth. Or worse, "How was your day?"

So it was good she'd reminded him that he signed her paycheck.

He went upstairs to the master bedroom and changed out of his suit into jeans and a cotton shirt. Then he quietly slipped into his son's room to check on him. Light from the hall picked out the small body curled up and sound asleep in the race car bed. Gavin crossed the room and bit back an oath when his bare foot found the sharp horns on the triceratops Sean had dropped on the floor. He stooped to pick it up and set it on the nightstand.

After dropping a soft kiss on his child's dark head, Gavin went down to the kitchen. There was a placemat on the table with silverware and a napkin. A bowl of lettuce with quartered tomatoes, sliced cucumbers and shredded carrots tossed with dressing sat in front of it. Wearily, he lowered himself into the chair.

M.J. was just lifting something out of the microwave and glanced over her shoulder. "Is he asleep?"

"Yeah. Remind me to have a talk with him about picking up toys."

Understanding gleamed in her eyes as she set the steaming plate of lasagna in front of him. "One of the dinosaurs escaped?"

"The one with the pointy things on its head."

"Better known as horns?"

He laughed. "Yeah. They hurt."

She sat down across from him. "Gavin, remember to talk to Sean about picking up his toys."

"Okay. That was helpful."

Humor shimmered in her eyes and stirred his anticipation. The stress and strains of the day slipped away as they talked and he found himself wondering what she would say next. Would she challenge him? Or make him laugh?

The give-and-take was comfortable.

He chewed on his salad and a thought occurred to him. After swallowing, he said, "Actually, you have been more helpful than I ever dreamed."

"You're not talking about heating pasta and making a salad," she guessed.

"No. Thanks to you, I'm able to have a conversation with my son. We're still a little rough around the edges, but we're doing it."

She folded her hands as she met his gaze. "He's coming along well. He missed you at dinner."

"I missed him, too." This was the first time in weeks Gavin hadn't made it home in time. That was thanks to M.J., too. She'd made him aware that he had more responsibility in parenting than simply providing the environment. "We talked on the phone. He didn't quite understand that the marketing meeting ran late."

"Give him time. He's only six."

"What, no disapproval for phoning in fatherhood?"

She looked sheepish. "Perhaps I was a bit harsh. I tend to have tunnel vision where kids are concerned. I do understand that you have responsibilities."

"Yeah."

But Gavin was beginning to realize that this slight, deceptively plain woman had made changes in his life. He wasn't sure if he was at all comfortable with that.

"It's getting late," he said. "You don't have to keep me company."

"Are you trying to get rid of me?" she teased.

Actually he was, but since he couldn't explain why, teasing was the way to go. "Of course not. I just don't want you to think you have to stay. If you have something important to do."

Her expression was wry. "You mean, like that bestselling thriller I'm reading?"

"No hot date?"

"Oh, please. Have you seen any men beating a path to the door?"

The innocent banter was like a smack upside his head. She didn't have a personal life. He ate half the lasagna before he asked, "Why don't you date? You're an attractive woman."

"Have you had your eyes examined recently?" She shifted in her seat across from him.

"There's nothing wrong with my eyes." He finished off his salad and never looked away. "Does it have anything to do with your husband?"

"No." The answer was a little too quick, too automatic. Too sharp. "When do I have time to meet anyone?" she added quickly, as if she heard the tone. "I'm a high school substitute teacher."

"Not at the moment."

"Which makes it even more of a challenge to meet someone." She toyed with a strand of hair, nervously twisting it around her finger.

An irrational surge of possessiveness swept through him. He didn't like the idea of her looking for guys. How stupid was that? He knew better, but the idea of her meeting men made him want to run interference and keep her from being taken advantage of. His feelings were all about protecting not possessing. "You're a young woman. Single." Lonely? "It hasn't occurred to me how isolated you are here."

"I don't feel that way."

"Young or isolated?" he asked.

"Both." Shadows shifted in her eyes. She was thinking about her son.

She'd been through every parent's worst nightmare. Gavin knew that because he was a parent and what he'd been through had been a nightmare. His child was getting better, but Gavin knew the trauma, the worry, the strain of the ordeal had aged him.

She met his gaze. "Sean talked about his mother today."

Hell of a segue. Obviously she didn't want to talk about herself. "I answered his question as best I could."

She nodded. "He told me his mother loves him, but she has things to do and knows his dad is taking good care of him."

"He seemed okay with that?"

"Yeah." She thought about it. "He sort of shared that in passing, then let it go. Didn't seem to me that he was dwelling on it."

"Good."

"Probably it will come up again. Hopefully not for a long time."

"Hopefully."

And who would he brainstorm an answer with then? M.J. would be gone.

She stood and reached for his empty dishes. "I'll take care of this."

"Thanks."

He watched the sway of her hips as she walked to the sink, and his gaze dropped to her legs. Desire rippled through him again and his body came to life as a pulse of need rushed through him. He didn't like it.

"I'm going upstairs," he said.

Standing at the sink, she glanced over her shoulder. "Okay. Good night. I'll see you in the morning."

He told himself he wasn't retreating. Removing himself was the sensible thing to do, because if she'd come close again, he'd have pulled her into his arms. And acting on his feelings would be stupid and foolish. He hated that he always questioned. She'd said it herself—she had to make a living. But Gavin had the means to provide a luxurious lifestyle.

Except if she was trying to get money out of him, she wasn't using any of the feminine tricks he'd encountered before. And he'd encountered a lot. She was simply good to his son. Pleasant, funny, sassy—the whole package. Sexy in a way that sneaked up on a man.

That didn't mean he could afford to lose control. Lust was pouring through him, but that was safe. It was different from need. He wouldn't need a woman he couldn't trust. M.J. had always caved to his demands when he increased the dollar amount. Except when she'd agreed to let him rehire her.

But that could be part of her plan. Giving him a false sense of security. How could he believe she wasn't looking for a way to manipulate him? He wouldn't be made a fool of again. He wouldn't need her.

Needing someone had never worked for him.

Chapter Twelve

"Are you sure you don't mind Sean being here so much?" M.J. glanced over her shoulder at the child helping her mother arrange roses in a vase. "He insisted on coming again."

"We love having him," Aunt Lil assured her. She washed the cookie sheet and handed it over for drying.

"But it's been three or four times a week," M.J. protested.

"So we're the party house for the six-year-old set?" The older woman's eyes twinkled.

M.J. laughed. "He likes the attention, and it's obviously good for him."

Evelyn let Sean put the last rose in the vase. "It's perfect," she assured him.

The little boy beamed at the praise, then looked up expectantly. "Now what can I do?"

Aunt Lil shook her head. "Does he ever rest?"

"Only when he's asleep," M.J. said fondly.

"I wish I could siphon off some of that energy. He makes me tired just watching him, but Ev and I love having him here. It keeps the house from being too quiet."

"That's the truth," her mother agreed, stopping in the doorway with the flowers in her hands. "I'm going to put these on the dining room table. Get Sean some apple juice, will you, M.J.? All that activity makes a boy thirsty."

"Coming right up."

"I'll be back in a minute with something to keep him occupied."

M.J. opened the refrigerator and grabbed the juice container, then poured it into a glass she took from the cupboard. She carried it over to where he sat, elbow on the table, chin in palm, sneaker-clad feet dangling back and forth.

"Here you go, Seanster."

After taking the glass, he sipped, then set it down right in front of him.

M.J. automatically moved it farther out of his reach so those active little limbs couldn't knock it over. Funny, she thought, how a mother never forgot things like that. When her Brian had toddled, she'd instinctively put her hand between his head and sharp edges of tables at the same level, to keep him from bumping. She'd learned to anticipate and sometimes save him from getting hurt. If only she'd been there that day, maybe... But the key word was sometimes.

Her chest squeezed tight. There was no way to anticipate and avoid that regret. She brushed her hand across Sean's soft hair. He looked up, his dark eyes shining, and smiled. This child was alive and thriving, and that was a blessing. She couldn't bring her son back, but making a difference in Sean's life felt really good.

"This will be fun." Her mother walked back into the room with a stack of colored pencils, crayons, coloring books and blank white paper and set them down on the table.

At first M.J. thought her mom had bought supplies for Sean, but when she looked closer her stomach dropped. Some of the pencils were just nubs, having been sharpened many times. Most of the crayons were broken, blunt, the paper covering the wax sticks torn back from much use. As Sean turned the book's pages, she could see many dinosaurs had been colored and not inside the lines. Consistent with a four-year-old.

She looked at her mother. "Are these Brian's?"

Evelyn's eyes were sad as she looked at the pictures her grandson had worked on. "I couldn't throw them away. I hope you don't mind."

"I don't." M.J. swallowed. "Sean will enjoy using them."

M.J. joined her aunt at the sink and the two of them watched as Sean picked a page to color and her mother worked on the one beside it. Their heads were close together as they concentrated.

"Having him here is good for all of us," her aunt said.

M.J. nodded. "No matter how much we sometimes wish it didn't, life does go on."

"And eventually we find a reason to go on, too."

"I'm learning that," M.J. said.

Lil smiled. "Now I'm going to watch my soap opera. That's senior speak for 'taking a nap.'"

"Enjoy," M.J. said as her aunt left. She walked over and stood behind Sean. "Nice work, kiddo. I like that blue tree."

"Look how well he stays in the lines," Evelyn complimented. "And he added a big yellow sun."

"Can I take it home to show Daddy?"

"Of course. I'll tear it out for you," Evelyn said.

"I can do it." He pulled the book from her with typical boyish energy and helpful enthusiasm.

The domino effect was in motion before M.J. could anticipate and react. The book hit the box of crayons and knocked it into the glass of juice, toppling it and sending the liquid streaming across the table to drip off and onto the opposite chair.

"Uh-oh." Evelyn jumped up.

Sean's eyes grew wide and stricken as he slid off his chair. "I didn't throw anything."

"It's all right." Her mother patted his shoulder. "Let's wipe it up before it gets sticky. Good boys clean up their messes."

M.J. heard the words and tensed. She was still

dealing with the effects of that message. How would Sean take it? After hurrying to get a roll of paper towels and a wet dishrag, she handed them to her mother.

She went down on one knee in front of the little boy who was looking guilty and uncertain. M.J. hugged him tight, then looked at him. "You're a good boy, Sean. Accidents happen. It wasn't your fault. Do you understand?"

He nodded and pointed to his chest. "Big boy."

She grinned. "Now why don't you go wash your hands and we'll have a snack before we go home and see your daddy."

"Okay." He ran out of the room.

M.J. stood and met her mother's questioning gaze. "I know you weren't being unkind, but cleaning up a mess has nothing to do with him being a good boy."

"I wasn't being judgmental," Evelyn defended. "It's what my mother always said—like clean your plate because people are starving in the world. It was something I was always told."

And passed on, M.J. thought. Like Gavin's negative parenting style. But they'd talked about it and he was working on it. M.J. had always tried to be good because she wanted her mother's love and approval. She cleaned up her messes because that's what good girls did. But love shouldn't have conditions.

"Mom, you're right that Sean needs to learn to clean up. But it should be about building character, not a moral issue."

Evelyn frowned, her feelings obviously hurt. "It was an innocent remark."

M.J. stacked the coloring supplies, then mopped up the spill. With the wet rag, she finished off the job so the juice wouldn't dry sticky.

She saw the distress in her mother's eyes and was sorry for it. But this was important. "Sometimes innocent remarks can do a lot of damage."

"I don't know what you mean."

"Okay. Let me give you an example. I worked with a family and while the five-year-old was going through therapy, his grandmother was diagnosed with cancer. When they brought her to live with them, the little guy threw a temper tantrum. His grandmother could see how upsetting it was to his mother and was trying to calm him. She told him when he yelled it made her head hurt. Innocent remark."

"What happened?"

"When his grandmother died five months later and they told him as gently as possible, he asked if she died because he yelled."

Her mother looked shocked as the ramifications sank in. "My God, if he hadn't said anything—"

"He might grow up thinking he was responsible for his grandmother's death," M.J. confirmed.

Her mother sat down. As their gazes locked, awareness crept into her eyes. "This isn't all about Sean, is it?"

"No. When I was a little girl, I heard what you said to Aunt Lil. That my father left for someone better."

She gasped. "Oh, M.J.—I never meant for you to know about that."

"I understand." She brought the trash can to the table and dropped the wet paper towels into it. "But on top of that, you passed on to me what Grandma said to you. 'Good girls clean up their messes.' It all mixed up for me. If I wasn't good enough, you'd leave."

Evelyn reached out and took her hand. "Oh, honey. I'm so sorry you got that impression. I'd never have left you. I love you."

"The adult me knows that. The little girl—" She shook her head. "It's such a small thing, really, what we say to children and think is harmless. And we have no idea how they process the information. For me that meant cleaning up my mess without making waves. And that way wasn't always the best way."

"You're talking about marrying Vince because you were pregnant, aren't you?"

"You knew?" Shocked, M.J. sank into the chair beside her mother's.

"I'm old, not blind." The smile was wry, then turned sad. "I could see there was trouble between you way before he died."

"You never said anything."

"I didn't want to interfere. I thought you knew you could come to me with anything." Evelyn took M.J.'s hand into both of her own. "I'm here for you, sweetie."

M.J. smiled and nodded. She knew her mother meant what she said, but she couldn't tell her about the financial mess. It was her own poor judgment in men that was responsible. She was fixing it and there was no reason her mother had to worry.

Sean raced back into the room. "I want—picture. I want to show Aunt Lil. I'm taking it— Take it home for my daddy."

"Your daddy will love it, Sean." M.J. handed it to him and said, "If Aunt Lil is sleeping, be very quiet and come back. Okay?" He nodded, then ran out again.

Evelyn watched him. "His speech is really coming along."

"Yeah. He's doing very well. When school starts in a few weeks, he'll be mainstreamed back into the classroom. The district SLP will work with him and monitor his progress."

Which meant her time was almost up. The realization startled her. She was going to miss Sean. And Gavin. A hollow, empty feeling opened up inside her that was worse than the pain.

"What are you going to do then?" her mother asked.

She couldn't reveal the financial crisis to her mother, but she could share something else. "I've decided to go back to speech pathology."

"I'm glad, M.J." Her mother's smile chased away the lingering hurt. She squeezed M.J.'s hand. "Good for you."

"Yeah." She remembered what she'd said to Gavin. "I can't bring Brian back. But I can work with kids and for me that will help keep his memory alive."

"Kids like Sean."

"I never thought I'd be grateful to Gavin for talking me into doing it. But I am."

"And how is your millionaire?" Evelyn asked.

"Not mine, for one thing." And she just barely stopped herself from wishing he could be.

"But—" Evelyn prompted.

"But nothing."

"Then why are you blushing? You look just like you did when you were a little girl and in trouble."

M.J. felt the warmth in her cheeks. "Things are troubling," she admitted.

"By 'troubling,' I assume you mean the fact that when you two are in the same room you set off more sparks than a fried electrical circuit."

M.J. didn't have any idea it had been that obvious. She just knew she looked forward to seeing him every day. When they were in the same room she felt hot all over and completely alive. The night she'd sat in the kitchen while he ate, she'd been happy just being with him. And she remembered the dark intensity on his face when he'd abruptly walked out. For just a moment his gaze had lingered on her mouth, the look as physical as a kiss.

The memory was so vivid, she shivered now as she had then. They'd talked about her lack of a personal life. Between running a multimillion dollar company and raising his son, he didn't have one, either. But she didn't delude herself. If there was any attraction on his part, it was because he was lonely and she was handy. That would change soon enough, when her SLP services were no longer needed.

"He's a nice man and a good father. But there's not now, nor will there ever be, anything between us." She squeezed her mother's hand, then pulled her own away. "My life isn't a governess-and-the-millionaire romance novel."

When the tea didn't relax M.J. enough to sleep, she set aside her book, got out of bed and put on her short robe over her knit camisole and cotton pajama bottoms. The earlier scene with her mother had dredged up so many memories—some precious, some painful, some that made her angry at her husband's betrayal. Maybe another cup of chamomile would help her rest.

She quietly left her suite at the far end of the house and tiptoed past Sean's room, peeking in to make sure he was all right. He was sleeping the sleep of the innocent, she thought. His dark head, tufts of hair sticking out of the blankets, tugged at her heart. Before stepping out of his room, she couldn't resist dropping a light kiss on his forehead and felt the fragile tenderness growing inside her.

The house was dark and quiet, but a dim light on each stair illuminated the way. In the kitchen, she turned on the subdued light beneath the cupboards, then put a tea bag in her cup, filled it with water and slid it into the microwave. While she waited for it to heat, she looked at the refrigerator beside her and noticed Sean's coloring book page with its blue tree and big sun attached to a magnet that read, "Look What I Made."

She traced the yellow slashes that were a little boy's ray of sunshine and colored with her son's crayons. Tears filled her eyes. She would always miss Brian. She'd always blame herself for what happened to him. Suddenly the recessed lights overhead blazed on and she turned.

"M.J.?" Gavin stood in the doorway, shirtless.

It looked like he'd hastily thrown on jeans, because the button was unfastened. Her mouth went dry at the sight of him. His dark hair was rumpled, a little out of control, which was different for him—and oh, so sexy. A dusting of dark hair sprinkled across his chest to taper over his flat belly and disappear into the open vee at his waistband, hinting at the masculinity she couldn't see. Long muscular legs encased in denim led to bare feet. She'd never before thought about a man's feet being sexy, but she did now. Because this was the first time she'd seen Gavin like this.

The heat he generated in her was almost enough to dry her tears. But not quite. She turned away before he could see them and pulled her robe closed, tying it securely.

And then he was behind her, hands on her arms, turning her back to face him. "You're crying."

"I am?" She touched her cheek and felt the wetness. Her mouth had gone dry. Her eyes? Not so much.

"What's wrong?" Concern was etched on his

features, but as his gaze dropped to her chest, they caught fire.

She shook her head. "I couldn't sleep. I'm getting a cup of tea." The beeping appliance signaled it was done, confirming her words. "I'll just go back up now. Sorry if I disturbed you."

"You didn't. I couldn't sleep, either."

It was on the tip of her tongue to ask what his excuse was, but that would lead to questions, sharing, and she didn't want that. She took her steaming mug from the microwave. The handle was too hot to hold and she set it down on the counter and shook her hand. "Would you like some chamomile?"

"I was thinking of something a little stronger."

When he took a step forward, she retreated slightly and felt the refrigerator against her back. With his index finger, he lightly traced the tracks of her tears. "Why are you crying?"

This was such a big kitchen, she thought. When did all the air disappear? But she knew. Fire needs oxygen to burn and the moment the smoldering look fired in his eyes, she couldn't breathe.

"I'm okay. I'll just go back up now—"

He was directly in front of her, so close, her thin knit nightclothes didn't shield her from the heat of his body. The open tab of his jeans scraped the tie of her robe.

"Talking about it might help you sleep. Maybe better than some nasty-tasting dried leaves in a cup of hot water."

"And liquor that burns all the way to your belly is so much more pleasing to the palate?"

"It's an acquired taste."

So was he, she thought. She hadn't liked him at first. But he'd grown on her. Too much.

With his knuckle, he nudged her chin up until their gazes locked. "What's keeping you awake?"

Besides thoughts of him? She sighed, suddenly tired and unwilling to fight his determination. "It was a bad day. Something with my mom."

"Sean?"

She shook her head and felt the tears burn again. Gavin's image wavered. "He's a terrific kid."

When another tear fell, Gavin gathered her into his arms and she slid her arms around his waist, her palms flat on the smooth skin of his back. Her breasts throbbed against the solid, warm wall of his chest— the only thing between her flesh and his a thin layer of knit cotton. His heart was beating very fast and her own picked up the cadence. He felt so solid and safe, and she wanted to stay right here forever.

She wanted it too much, and that was why she needed to get away.

Pushing gently against him, she said, "Gavin, I—"

He moved slightly, but didn't let her go. She could see the desire in his eyes and it sucked all the air from her lungs. He cupped her face in his hands and tunneled his fingers in her hair as his body held her backed against the refrigerator.

He touched his mouth to hers and she burst into

flame. He traced her top lip with his tongue and she opened to him, wanting the mindlessness he could give her. The things he did shredded her breathing and his until the ragged sounds twined together and filled the room.

He lifted his head and stared, his eyes never leaving hers. He braced his hands on either side of her head and pressed his body to hers, making it impossible for her to miss his arousal. He wanted her. The sheer wonder of that realization went to her head and made her his willing captive.

"I've tried to make it go away. But I can't. I want you," he confirmed with words. His voice was gruff, the message blunt. No sweet coaxing or promises.

And that was fine with her. She wanted him, too, and the feeling was so big it pushed out any other thoughts. Which was exactly what she needed.

Their gazes danced and took each other's measure until she could only nod her surrender. In a heartbeat, her hand was in his and he was leading her upstairs.

Inside the master suite, he closed and locked the door. She'd seen the room, but never through the eyes of intimacy. The mahogany four-poster bed matched the armoire—big, dark, bold—like the man. It was decorated in earth tones with black accents—also like the man. It was exciting—the essence of the man. The comforter and blankets were thrown back as if he'd been restless and frustrated. One brass lamp was on, the lighting subdued.

Gavin settled his hands at her waist and lowered

his mouth to hers, teasing, tasting, exploring. She rested her palms on his flat abdomen, then slid them up. His chest hair was coarse, stimulating as she skimmed the contours. He sucked in a breath when she grazed a nipple and it tightened responsively.

"Two can play," he said, his tone gravel and whiskey.

With one quick flick of his fingers, he'd untied her robe, then brushed it off her shoulders. Her camisole was the next target of his extraordinary attention. He slid one finger beneath the skinny strap and eased it over her shoulder, exposing her breast. When he cupped her in his warm palm, a flood of desire surged through her. He fanned the flames as he gently kneaded her flesh, then brushed his thumb back and forth over her nipple. It pebbled at the touch.

"Two can definitely play." Did that ragged, breathy, needy voice actually belong to her?

He put his hands at her waist, took the hem of the camisole and in one movement, pulled it up and over her head, then tossed it aside. She felt cool air on her shoulders and breasts along with Gavin's approving gaze. The look of desire heated her and seemed to dissolve her legs from the knees down. When she staggered, he was there and swung her into his arms, their faces inches apart.

His dark eyes seared into her. "You do something to me, Mary Jane Taylor. I'm not sure I like it, but I can't seem to change it. So, I've decided to go with it."

She knew precisely what he meant and the words were more seductive than empty flattery. She wasn't beautiful. She knew that. She was what she was and tonight that was enough.

"I feel the same way."

If his words were exactly right, his lips when he took hers were even more right. With her in his arms, he walked to the bed, kissing her thoroughly. Then he set one knee on the mattress and placed her gently in the center of it. He stepped back and unzipped his jeans. When the denim parted, his impressive erection sprang free. Her pulse jumped and her heart hammered as she held out her arms in invitation.

In two seconds he was naked and stretched out beside her, pulling her to him. The feel of warm skin to warm skin was more intoxicating than wine, more seductive than moonlight and roses. With one hand he swept off her pajama bottoms, then splayed his fingers over her belly. Muscles quivered and jumped, and she parted for him.

He teased the curls at the juncture of her thighs as he kissed her eyes, nose, chin and neck. When he touched his tongue to a spot just beneath her ear, heat exploded inside, making her writhe beneath his touch. He slid one finger into her waiting wetness as he searched and found the feminine nub where all the nerve endings concentrated. Her last coherent thought was gratitude for his determination and attention to detail.

Then the intense pleasure his friction created grew too much and she shattered while lights went off like fireworks behind her eyes. The shudders seemed to go on forever, and when they subsided she found her forehead resting against his chest.

He gently scraped his teeth on her earlobe and whispered, "That was quite an explosion."

"It's been a while," she said breathlessly.

"So not what a man wants to hear," he joked.

"If you're fishing for a compliment, I'd have to say, on a scale of one to ten, that was fifteen plus."

"Better."

His eyes were teasing, but need lurked around the edges. M.J. rested her hand on the smooth, naked skin of his shoulder then kissed the path she'd traced with her finger. Then, as if he was the president and CEO of sex, he took over and led the way until their ragged breathing mingled and rational thought fled.

He eased her onto her back, then reached across her and opened the nightstand. He rooted through and pulled out a square packet, tearing it open with his teeth. After rolling the condom over himself, he turned on his side and their bodies were pressed together, his erection jutting into her thigh. After kissing her thoroughly, he sucked on her lower lip, then traced her ear with the tip of his tongue. She gasped out a moan as desire built inside her until she couldn't stand it.

"Please," she whispered.

That was all he needed. He settled her on her back and entered in one swift thrust, then grew still as he let her grow accustomed to the feel of him inside her. She curved her hand around his strong neck and drew his head down, touching her lips to his. When he rested his forearms on either side of her, his breathing was harsh and fast. He began to move, slowly at first, then increasing as her hips, her body, picked up the rhythm.

Her passion built again, something she hadn't thought possible. Then he slid a hand between them as he moved and found the nub, pleasuring it with his thumb. Again tension built until it was shattered by a brilliant blast and she broke apart into what felt like a million pieces of light. He thrust one last time and sucked in air, his body convulsing then going still as he groaned out his release.

When he was spent, he touched his forehead to hers, then kissed her tenderly. "That was amazing."

"An understatement."

He rolled away and off the bed, leaving her as he disappeared into the bathroom. Her body was like a limp rag and before she could pull herself together and figure out how to handle the awkward aftereffects, Gavin returned. He slid into bed, then gathered her to him, and it wasn't awkward at all. It was lovely.

He kissed her forehead and said, "Now I'd like you to tell me what happened today to make you cry." He must have felt her tense because he added, "And I won't take no for an answer."

She knew he wouldn't. This was the downside of determination.

Chapter Thirteen

Gavin tamped down his impatience as he waited for her to tell him what was wrong. Seeing her cry had made him determined to find out what made her sad and try to make it better.

"It was one of those days when the memories came out of nowhere," M.J. began. She pulled the sheet up over her breasts and tucked it beneath her arms. "It turns out Mom had saved Brian's coloring things and brought them out for Sean to play with."

"The picture he gave me was from one of Brian's coloring books, wasn't it?" Gavin asked, brushing the hair off her cheek.

"One of the dinosaur ones. They were his favorite." Her voice was laced with warmth, but the sadness was there, too.

"M.J., I—"

"It's okay," she reassured him. "I was fine with it. Those are good memories. Brian was sweet and generous. He always shared his things. It wasn't about that."

"Then what?"

"Sean spilled his juice and my mother said something. Not mean or anything. Just that good boys clean up their messes. It seemed I heard that a lot when I was growing up." She met his gaze and said, "Except it was about good girls."

"I figured." He'd just experienced her feminine charms for himself. And it was all good.

She skimmed her hand over his chest. "Anyway, the words touched a nerve and I talked to her about it. I told her the message I heard from the words was that you clean up your mess without asking for help. Sometimes you need help."

"What did she say?"

She sighed. "That she knew I was referring to the fact Vince and I got married because I was pregnant. I thought it was the best solution, but it wasn't. I'd have been better off alone."

Gavin remembered their conversation after Sean had wanted to know about his mother. M.J. had asked him what kind of man would pay a woman rather than let her terminate the life of an unborn child. He'd never once regretted what he did and was grateful for his son and the second chance at life M.J. had given him. She'd made a choice, too, and picked life with her child's father. Her words were tinged with absolute conviction and he was damn curious to know why she regretted marrying.

"Why would you have been better off alone?"

"Because I don't think I ever loved him. We met in college. There was an attraction and we went too fast. Then I was pregnant and we had a decision to make. Mom said she knew why I married Vince."

"You never talked to her about being pregnant?"

"Not until after the wedding. And today she told me she could see that things weren't… That the marriage was in trouble before he…before he died."

When she slipped out of his arms, Gavin missed her warmth, but he let her go. She held the sheet to her breasts as she fluffed the pillow, then sat up and leaned against it. He did the same and their bare shoulders brushed, sending heat radiating through him. Light from the lamp beside the bed glinted off the gold in her hair and her cheeks were still flushed from the sex. He wanted her again. But this wasn't the time. It was her story and he had to let her tell it her way. Her fingers plucked at the sheet, broadcasting her tension, telling him she had a lot more to say before getting to the part that had made her cry.

"So your mother knew you were having problems?" he encouraged.

M.J. nodded. "And she didn't know the worst of

it. Because I didn't know it then, either. Not until after Vince's accident."

"What was the worst?"

She glanced at him, then pulled her knees up to her chest and wrapped her arms around them, sheet and all. "He was a compulsive gambler."

Gavin wasn't sure what he expected, but definitely not that. This wasn't Vegas. It was the central coast of California. But as he thought about it, he realized there were ways to wager if one had a weakness for it. Horse races. Indian casinos. Sporting events from the World Series to the Super Bowl. You didn't even have to leave the house with online gambling.

He didn't know what to say, so he asked, "How did you find out?"

"He handled the money and I didn't have a clue what was going on. After he died, the calls started. Collection agencies. I got bills in the mail for credit cards I didn't know he had and all of them were maxed out. Apparently he was able to juggle everything while he was still working." Anger vibrated in her voice.

"What did he do? I mean, for a living."

She tilted her head and met his gaze. "Financial consultant. Ironic, huh?"

No comment. "You said *while* Vince was working."

She rested her chin on her knees. "After we lost Brian, he went into a deep depression. He slept a lot. Didn't go to work."

"That's not surprising." Gavin had come dangerously close to losing his own son. He didn't even want to imagine how it would actually feel.

"I know. It was a horrible time. I gave him his space. Although, it wasn't a conscious decision. The truth is, I was numb and grieving myself. We didn't talk. Until his company finally had to let him go. I suggested he get some help for his grief and we fought about it. He left the house, angry. That was the last time I saw him. He had an accident. Single car. He hit a tree and was killed instantly."

Gavin wanted to say he was sorry and remembered feeling this way when she'd told him about losing her son. Then he'd thought the attempt at comfort pathetic and that was before knowing how deep the trauma went. Now that he knew, it would be beyond pathetic.

The eyes she turned on him were haunted and angry—without a hint of the sorrow he'd seen earlier. The look on her face in the kitchen had twisted him in knots and he couldn't stop himself from pulling her into his arms. The feel of her against him. Her arms sliding around his waist. Her warmth and sweetness. All of it conspired against him and he couldn't put aside his wanting her. He would deal with that later. Now he still wanted to know what had put the tears in her eyes.

"What memory made you cry?"

"I don't think I can even say it out loud," she whispered.

"Maybe it's time." He pulled her out of her protective ball and into his arms, pressing her cheek to his chest. "Maybe you need to tell someone. Who better than me? You know my secrets. I've got no room to judge."

"It's my fault."

What did she mean? The gambling? Vince's death? Then he knew because the tone in her voice was absent the anger and filled with the horror of losing her son. "You mean, Brian's accident."

"Yes." The anguish in the single word was heart-breaking. "It was Saturday and I didn't usually work, but Vince encouraged me. Said he and Brian could use some male bonding time. Now I know it was probably all about the money," she said bitterly. "Apparently, Brian wandered out of the backyard when Vince was supposed to be watching him. I'm pretty sure when my baby ran into the street in front of that car, his father was online checking his bets. Later… After…" She swallowed hard. "I was turning off the computer. I saw numbers and games from an online casino site but I didn't understand. I was too numb with grief to know or care. But when the harassing phone calls started, I put it all together."

"I don't get it. How does that make anything your fault? Brian's father was taking care of him." Gavin had his own guilty secret and it was too close for comfort.

"It's my fault because I *wasn't* there." The self-recrimination in her tone ripped at his heart. "I should have been with Brian. I should have watched him. I wouldn't have let him out of my sight. But I was working. I was helping other children when my son needed me."

He felt the hot tears on his bare chest just before the sobs wrenched her slight body. Gavin held her while she cried. Finally he had an inkling why she'd so strenuously resisted this job in the beginning. Offering comfort the best way he knew how was the least he could do for bullying her back into the profession that had become too painful for her.

He wished he could do more than hold her. He wished he could make it all better. It was a dangerous feeling.

"Shh, M.J." He tightened his hold.

"Why didn't I see it? Why didn't I know what Vince was doing?" she sobbed.

"Because he was good at hiding it." Gavin rested his cheek on the top of her head. "Because you had no reason to be suspicious."

"But if I'd looked at everything harder—"

"Don't," he advised. "You'll make yourself crazy doing this." When she continued to cry, he said softly, "M.J., it's all right."

"It's n-not," she said brokenly. "And it never will be. A good mother keeps her child safe. I'm a horrible mother."

"No. I've seen you with Sean and what you do isn't all about the job. There's a way about you that makes you good at what you do." Gavin had seen for himself that her professional reputation was well-deserved. Nurturing came naturally to her. "I know what a horrible mother looks like and it's not you. The woman who gave me Sean fits the horrible profile. She didn't give a damn about him. Never gave a thought to being a parent. You're blaming yourself for something that happened when you weren't even there. What happened to Brian was a tragic accident. You've had lots of time to look back and figure out what you'd do differently. That's human. I do it, too. And don't think you have the market cornered on guilt."

She leaned away and looked at him, her eyes red-rimmed and puffy. "What does that mean?"

He hated thinking about this, let alone saying it out loud. But confession was in the air tonight. "I was home with Sean—the day he fell and hit his head." He pulled her tightly against him again. "He begged me to play catch and I told him I was busy. The thing is, he'd been told time and again not to play on the rocks, not to go down to the beach alone. But he did it anyway that day. Now I know it was about him trying to get my attention. If you think I don't feel guilty—"

"You're giving him time now," she said.

"Thanks to you not letting up on me until I got the message." He rubbed his hand up and down her arm. "Regrets come with the territory. I feel guilty, too."

"Don't feel bad, Gavin. Feel lucky. You got another chance with your son. You learned and changed. You're making him a priority." She sighed. "If anything, because of you and Sean, I learned, too. I got another chance. I'm not hiding anymore."

"And where were you hiding?"

"High school." There was the barest hint of humor cutting the tension in her voice.

"There are better places to take cover than refereeing fights and dodging fists."

"It's not that bad. And it pays pretty well."

"If it didn't, no one would go there."

She smiled. "I'm going there for a while until I get back into speech therapy and build up my client list. I still have a lot of debt to pay off."

And that explained why she'd worked two jobs before. Anger swept through him at the injustice. "It's your husband's debt."

"Husband. As in, we were married. That makes it my debt now," she said simply. "I have no choice."

"You know what you said before? About not asking for help to clean up a mess?" He tucked her hair behind her ear. "Maybe it's time to say something to your mother."

Instantly her body tensed. "No. I worry about her health. She had a mild heart attack a couple years ago. Besides, she's retired and on a fixed income. There's nothing she can do. I don't want to involve her. I'll take care of it."

The hell of it was Gavin didn't know whether to respect her spirit and independence or wonder if he was somehow part of her plan to take care of the mess. From the moment he'd met her he suspected she needed money and now knew why. It wasn't her fault, but that didn't change anything.

He was drawn to M.J.; he wanted her again. He'd seen past her exterior to the smart, funny, intuitive woman inside who could bring him to his knees. It was a good thing Sean was going back to school soon and they would no longer need her.

If one woman hadn't used his desire for profit, he wouldn't doubt the one in his arms. He could never regret having Sean, but he *had* been used. He'd been made a fool of. No matter how much M.J. tempted him, he wouldn't put himself in a position to repeat that failure.

Several weeks later the time had come to leave Cliff House. M.J. sat beside Sean on the family room floor between the sofa and the coffee table. They were drawing pictures and coloring while she waited for Henderson to drive her home for the last time. Her bags were packed and sitting by the front door.

"Are you excited about going back to school, kiddo?" She drew a stick figure on her paper.

"Yes. But I want you to stay here. At my house."

"I know."

He'd made his feelings clear when she and Gavin had prepared him a couple days earlier for the fact that it was time for her to leave. That was why she'd suggested this activity. He could get his feelings out, use drawing as a coping skill for his frustrations. The school district speech therapist would set up regular sessions to work on his vocabulary and he'd be able to use words to express himself instead of acting out.

She glanced at him and the frown and tight line of his mouth made her chest hurt. So she went back to her own drawing. Sean wasn't the only one who needed to cope. It would be very unprofessional to give any hint of how hard this was for her.

"You'll be able to see your friends in school," she pointed out.

"And have recess?"

"That's right." They'd talked about this a lot. "You'll be able to play and do activities with the other kids."

"Daddy said he'll buy me a dinosaur lunch box."

"That will be fun," she said with more enthusiasm than she felt. "What do you want to take for lunch on the first day of school?"

She wanted him to look forward to all the fun stuff. This child was going to make a full recovery and she didn't want him to be sad.

She was sad enough for both of them.

"I want peanut butter and jelly," he said without hesitation.

"That's what I figured you'd say." She smiled. "Anything else?"

He thought for a moment and tapped the blue crayon on his forehead. "Chips. The brown ones."

"Barbecue?" she asked.

"Yes."

Not a surprise. That was his favorite lunch. "Are you going to buy milk in the cafeteria?"

He looked at her, his dark eyes serious. "Do I have to?"

Milk was not his favorite. "No. You can bring a boxed juice. But remember what we talked about?"

"I know." His sigh was so exaggerated, she was afraid he'd implode. "Milk makes my—"

"Bones," she said.

"Bones strong. And my teeth." He nodded for emphasis.

"Good. What about fruit? Are you going to take some?"

"Apple," he said. "In pieces."

He liked it cut into wedges. She looked at her drawing and made a jagged line through the heart she'd drawn on one of her stick figures.

"That sounds good," she said.

"What sounds good?"

M.J. looked up. "Gavin."

They'd said goodbye that morning and she hadn't thought she'd see him again.

"Daddy!" Sean jumped up and ran to his father.

Gavin squatted and hugged him. "Hi, buddy."

"I didn't expect to see you before I left," she said.

"I'm here to drive you home."

Hope sprouted inside her like a weed through a crack in concrete. "I thought Henderson was going to do that."

"That was the plan. But in case there's a melt-down," he said, inclining his head toward his son.

Of course he was there for Sean. It was the silver lining of this whole horrible ordeal. Now Gavin was aware of how important it was to be there for his child.

His being here had nothing to do with wanting to see her, she thought, her little bubble of hope imploding. It was stupid to think anything had changed. He'd kept his distance since the night they'd made love. As much as she wanted to, she couldn't blame him. The man was a gold-digger magnet and she'd told him about her problems. Why in the world would he believe she was sincerely starting to care about him?

"Me and M.J. are drawing." Sean ran back to the table and grabbed his paper. "See? It's you and me and M.J."

Gavin studied it and pointed. "Are we crying?"

Sean nodded. "M.J. said I should draw how I felt."

"Are you sad, Seanster?" Gavin's arm came around his son and gathered the boy close.

"Yes. Make her stay, Daddy."

"You like M.J. here?" he asked, and the boy nodded.

The man was capable of learning, she thought. He'd responded in a sympathetic yet noncommittal way. The man was something, and she'd be lying if she said it hadn't been wonderful staying here. She was taken care of. Gavin had been sympathetic and supportive. And the sex was pretty good, too. Better than good.

She'd never felt these feelings before, not with any man. Not even the man she'd married. Relying on Vince had simply landed her in more trouble and she was still paying the price. She knew the longer she was around Gavin, the greater the temptation to ignore her good intentions to stand on her own and not be dependent on someone again.

Gavin settled the boy on his knee. "M.J. can't stay with us any longer. She's going to help other little boys the way she helped you."

"She's gonna help kids with words?" he asked.

"That's right, kiddo." Pressing her palms on the coffee table, she pushed herself up and stood.

Gavin met her gaze. "You can visit her anytime you want."

"Absolutely—" Her voice caught.

This was tearing her apart. She was happy that Gavin was here in case Sean needed him, but she'd have much preferred that Henderson drive her home. The last time Gavin had seen her cry… She couldn't think about that.

When she was confident of getting the words out, she said, "I think it's time to go."

"Okay." Gavin set the boy on his feet and stood. "Do you have everything?" he asked her.

"I think so."

"Seanster," he said, putting his hand on the child's shoulder, "why don't you help me put M.J.'s things in the car?"

"Okay."

When the two of them were gone, M.J. took a last look around. She was going to miss Cliff House and everyone in it.

She glanced down at her drawing, then picked it up. "I have everything but my heart," she whispered.

She traced the crack in the heart she'd drawn. This was just what she'd been afraid of the first time she'd walked into this house. Children were resilient and in a week Sean wouldn't miss her. She wished she could say the same for herself and her feelings for the Spencer men. The depth of those feelings was a clear indication that she was leaving just in time.

The son had melted her heart. She was getting out before the father broke it.

Chapter Fourteen

Gavin stood on the porch outside M.J.'s house waiting for someone to answer the door. Henderson had dropped Sean off earlier to see her and they'd agreed Gavin would pick him up on his way home from work.

The door finally opened and M.J. was there. He hadn't seen her for over a week and it was as if something that was out of whack inside him clicked into place. He didn't like that and hoped the check he had for her would fix it.

"Gavin." She looked surprised to see him.

"Hi. Is something wrong?" Funny, just seeing her made everything feel right for the first time in days. "Sean?"

"He's fine," she quickly assured him. "But I called the house and talked to Henderson. Sean went to the movies with my mother and Aunt Lil." She shrugged. "They wanted to see the new animated feature that's out and told him they needed a kid for cover so it wouldn't look weird for two old ladies to be there."

"No one looks weird. Those stories are multilayered so adults and kids can both enjoy them."

"I know. More importantly, they know. But Sean thinks he's doing them a big favor. And he really wanted to go with them," she added, tucking her fingers into the pockets of her jeans. "They're going to drop him off after the show. He'll be home in time for dinner. I'm sorry you came out of your way."

Gavin was sorry, too. He could go on ignoring how much he'd missed her if he wasn't looking at her right now. He could continue to overlook how quiet the house seemed without her there. No one teased and challenged him. Or made him laugh. Except Sean, but that was different. No one with gold in her hair or eyes the color of a California sky on a summer day made him want to see what she'd say next. No one else made him wax poetic about hair and eye color. And he'd come here to get her out of his system.

"It wasn't out of my way."

"But that's not like Henderson to forget," M.J. said. "Should I worry?"

"He didn't forget. I wanted to pick up Sean." But Gavin had almost forgotten that she smelled like flowers and sunshine and the thought backed him up a step. He didn't trust himself too close to her. His hands tingled with the need to touch her. He wanted her in his arms, to cut the loneliness just for a few moments. "Thanks for letting him come by and visit."

She leaned a shoulder against the doorjamb. "We love having him here. Anytime. And you." Her voice dropped into the husky range. "Would you like to come in? For a cookie? They're fresh and they've got Sean Spencer's fingerprints all over them."

A corner of his mouth curved up. "He helped?"

"Are you kidding? Try and stop him. He's becoming quite the cookie expert, by the way."

"Then how can I say no?"

Even though common sense was urging him to do just that. But he couldn't seem to stop himself. Since the day he'd brought her home for good, he'd wandered around Cliff House with a vague sense that he'd lost something and couldn't find it. Something he badly needed. The moment she'd opened the door, he'd found whatever it was he'd been missing.

M.J. stepped back as he came inside. He stood in the same spot where Sean had asked about his mother. Later M.J. had talked him through the crisis. After being here, bad memories had closed in on her and he'd talked her through that.

Right after making love to her.

And he'd wanted her ever since. He'd never struggled with his concentration when he was involved with a woman, but he did now and they weren't exactly involved. He didn't like this out-of-control feeling.

M.J. closed the door and said, "Would you like some coffee?"

As she started to walk past him, Gavin took her arm. Touching the soft, satin flesh floored the pedal on his idling testosterone. "I'd like you."

Her gaze jumped to his and something hot and electric passed between them. "I'd like you, too," she said in that erotic voice that evoked visions of tangled sheets and exposed flesh.

Gavin tugged gently and she went eagerly into his arms, her face instinctively turned up for his kiss. He willingly obliged and took her lips, instantly tasting the heat that matched his own. He lingered over her mouth, drinking in the need as he realized the first touch was too much and the rest wouldn't be enough.

The scent of her was the same. The feel of her hadn't changed. Only the wanting was so much more than last time because now he knew the pleasure he would find in her.

He swept his hand from her waist to her breast, a firm, possessive stroke. Cupping her in his palm, he was suddenly desperate to feel her bare flesh. When he started to unbutton her shirt, he noticed his fingers were shaking.

She put her hand over his. "Not here. Upstairs."

Her voice was calm, rational, but her breathing was as uneven as his own. He found himself following her upstairs even as he was trying to resist this—

resist her. But his gaze was drawn to the sway of her hips, the curve of her butt, the way the denim hugged her thighs. Right now he was in danger of swallowing his own tongue and doubted he'd have noticed if he was walking barefoot over hot coals.

She led him into a room at the top of the stairs, then shut the door behind them. The desk, the bay window, everything around him blurred as his focus was drawn to the bed with the pink spread. He didn't think he'd ever seen anything more seductive. Not until he looked at M.J., undoing the tiny buttons on her cotton shirt.

He moved closer and took her hand, his thumb in her palm, pressing her knuckles up as he touched his lips to them. "Let me," he said.

One by one he released the buttons, watching the sides of her cotton blouse part and expose her white bra and the creamy flesh above and below it. In one smooth motion he slid his fingers over her shoulders and the material to the floor.

"You're beautiful," he said, looking into her eyes.

She started to reach behind her to unfasten the white cotton and he stopped her again. "Let me. Turn around."

She did and he easily undid the hooks. In a heartbeat she was all soft, smooth skin from the waist up. He curved his hands over her shoulders and pulled her back against his chest, then cupped her breasts in his palms. She fit him perfectly; she felt like heaven.

Heat exploded through him when she leaned her head back into his shoulder. Her eyelids drifted shut.

Her chest rose and fell rapidly as he kneaded the soft flesh in his hands. Her wanton pose presented to him the long, graceful column of her neck. The temptation was more than he could resist and he touched his lips to the spot just below her ear and drank in what she offered up. She sucked in a breath as he rubbed his thumbs over her erect nipples. Soft, helpless sounds deep in her throat pushed him over the edge.

He turned her and she reached out, her breathing ragged as she unbuttoned his shirt. He unbuckled his belt and unfastened his slacks. In a haze of frantic need, somehow they removed the rest of their clothes and swept back that pink bedspread.

They fell on the bed in a tangle of arms and legs and mouths. Their panting breath filled the room as the shadowy light of late afternoon reflected off the walls. He took her breast in his mouth, rolling his tongue over her nipple, feeling it harden under the attention he was lavishing.

At the same time he swept his hand over her ribs, across her flat belly, resting his palm there as he parted her feminine folds. He slid one finger into her wetness and heard her gasp of pleasure. His erection pulsed, hard and ready, at that mind-blowing point between pain and pleasure, as he ruthlessly pulled together the threads of his self-control.

With his thumb, he located the spot that drove her wild, then brushed his index finger over it in slow circles that had her writhing beneath his hand. Her hips lifted slightly, her body instinctively reaching for what he could give. He increased the speed and pressure until she sucked in a breath and went still, just before shudders racked her from head to toe. He held her until her release was over, kissing her eyes, her nose, her mouth.

When she slid her arms around his neck, he pressed her onto the mattress, his own need pounding through him, demanding that he be inside her. Automatically he reached out, but there was no nightstand. No condom. He groaned, then rolled away and off the bed.

"Gavin?" Her gaze questioned.

"Condom," was all he could manage.

"I don't have one."

"I do."

He fumbled for his pants and wallet, the protection he always kept there. When it was in place, he returned to her. From the foot of the bed, he moved forward—kissing her calf, her knee, her thigh, her belly and her breasts. Then he braced his hands on either side of her and entered her in one long smooth motion.

She was moist and ready and slid her hands up his arms to his shoulders. Dusky light bathed the smile on her face in a golden glow as she wrapped her silky legs around his waist. Her hips picked up the rhythm of his thrusts as he plunged deep again and again. Pressure built, grinding through him, demanding he let go. When he couldn't hold back anymore, the power of his release almost took the top of his head off.

He collapsed beside her and pulled her close,

savoring the feel of her arm across his abdomen and her slender body next to his. Eventually sanity returned with a vengeance and with it came all the doubts. Was it just chance that she'd been alone? She'd seemed surprised when he showed up, but was she really? Or had she manipulated the situation? Henderson would have called him about any change in plan.

And had she faked the way she'd responded to him? The only thing M.J. couldn't have known was how much he needed her. That had taken even him by surprise.

"This is the attic," M.J. said, leading Gavin up to the third floor of the house.

She glanced over her shoulder and smiled, still basking in the amazing post-lovemaking glow. She'd dozed in his arms, then reluctantly dressed before calling her mother's cell phone to leave the message that Gavin was waiting here at the house for Sean. Then Gavin had asked her to show him around.

The wooden floor creaked as they moved through the cluttered, rectangular room with the peaked roof. In the center, a string dangled and she pulled on it, lighting the bare bulb overhead. She glanced at the racks of clothes, boxes, the old form her great-grandmother had used to fit a dress or blouse she was sewing. There were shelves of books and a big leather trunk.

She opened it, revealing hats, dresses and crocheted shawls. "I used to play dress-up with these and pretend I was the lady of the manor when I was a little girl." She took his hand and tugged him into the corner by the shelves filled with toys and books. "These were mine."

She picked up the little pony with long, coarse hair and smiled at it. There was the collection of bears with hearts on their chests. Dolls. The miniature china tea set. Nearby was the little table where she'd arranged her stuffed animals for tea parties.

"Sean and I were up here today," she said.

One dark eyebrow rose. "Tell me he didn't play dress-up."

"He didn't," she said laughing. "He's all boy. The old train set caught his attention in a big way."

"That's a relief."

Gavin moved to a box overflowing with photograph albums. He lifted the cover on the top one and it came off in his hand. The pages inside were discolored and crumbling almost to dust. "Sorry," he said, meeting her gaze. "I had no idea it was so fragile."

"Don't worry about it."

That wasn't all that was fragile, she thought. Did he feel their connection? she wondered. She studied the serious, handsome line of his profile and her heart tilted, squeezing almost painfully. She felt something for this man, she realized, a new and delicate emotion.

If it wasn't clear by the way she'd missed seeing him every day, she got the message big-time when she'd opened the door and seen him standing there. It had taken every ounce of her self-control not to launch herself into his arms. Then he'd said he wanted her and she'd been lost. He was a good man. He was a man you could count on. But was he a man she could trust?

Maybe it was time to take a chance and trust him with everything.

"We keep meaning to do something about preserving these pictures," she said, taking the album cover from him. She turned it over, pointing out the faded writing on the other side. "This is my great-grandparents' wedding album." She set the album cover back in the box. "Right after they were married, my great-grandparents moved from New Jersey here to the central coast of California. They opened a store, made a modest amount of money and built this house."

"The Victorian lines and architecture are really special. The workmanship is solid."

"Yeah. This house means a lot to us. It's part of the fabric of my family." She tugged on the string and turned off the light, then led him downstairs into the kitchen. Looking around at the faded and chipped paint and cupboards that needed refinishing, she said, "I remember my mother tucking me into bed at night and telling me that we'd always have a roof over our head. No one could take it away from us. People come and go, but the land is forever and someday it would be mine."

Gavin stood in the doorway. "That's quite a legacy."

She nodded, then threw the old coffee filter and grounds into the trash. "My mother wants to die here."

He looked surprised. "I hope that wasn't part of the bedtime ritual."

"No." She took the pot and filled it with water then poured it into the coffeemaker. "She had a heart attack a couple years ago. Mild, but something like that makes you face some serious things."

"Yeah."

"She told me when her time comes, she doesn't want to be in the hospital. I'm not to take any extraordinary measures and she wants to be in this house where she grew up." She took a breath. "Thank God she recovered, but she made the mistake of putting the house in my name."

He frowned. "Mistake?"

M.J. measured grounds into the filter, then flipped the switch and heard the sizzle that signaled the coffee starting to drip.

She felt dirty confessing this, but secrets were destructive. It was time to let go. "Vince took out a mortgage against the property and forged my signature on the papers. Recently, I found out there's a second mortgage with a balloon payment. If I can't keep current, they could foreclose."

"Does your mother know?" Anger laced his words.

She shook her head. "And I don't want her to. She'd have another heart attack. And it comes down to the usual—"

"Little girls clean up their messes," he finished.

Her chest felt tight and emotion closed off her throat. She nodded miserably. Then Gavin gathered her into his arms. She slid her arms around his waist and rested her cheek against his chest, grateful to have his comforting strength. It was a relief to share the burden she'd been carrying by herself for so long.

They'd come a long way from that day in this very kitchen when she'd thought him obnoxious, aggressive, determined and controlling. Now she knew Gavin had simply been taking care of someone he loved, making sure his son had what he thought was the best. And she knew now that she'd fallen in love with him.

She sniffled and blinked away the tears. "Now you know the whole sad story."

"That's why you finally agreed to work with Sean," he guessed.

She felt the tension in him and lifted her gaze to his. "You said everyone has their price, but it's not that so much as I couldn't make ends meet. I just needed to work a little harder." She stepped away from him. "I was planning to start making arrangements for the repairs before losing Brian and my husband. Now I have to concentrate on paying back all of that debt."

"Your mother and aunt must notice."

"If they do, neither of them says anything. I'm going to keep my fingers crossed that they don't until I'm in a position to start restoring the place."

Gavin leaned a shoulder against the refrigerator and watched her. "I see."

M.J. studied him, wondering what he was thinking. She was torn between relief at confessing what she'd been going through and the uneasy feeling that he was on edge. It was probably just her imagination.

"Is something wrong?" she asked.

"No."

"Would you like some coffee? It'll be ready in a minute."

"No, thanks."

"Okay." She noticed tension around his mouth and the way he wouldn't meet her gaze.

M.J. needed to keep her hands busy. She took Great-Grandmother Anna's green Depression sandwich plate from the dining room buffet, arranged sugar and chocolate chip cookies on it, then placed it on the kitchen table. When she turned around Gavin had a piece of paper in his hand. A muscle in his cheek jerked as he stared at it.

"Gavin?" Something was wrong.

"I want you to have this," he said.

"What is it?" She took it and glanced down. It was a check made out to her, and her eyes widened when she saw the number of zeroes.

"It's a bonus for your work with Sean," he explained.

His father had paid off his mother. He'd paid Sean's mother a bonus to sign away her rights. She looked into his eyes and knew he would never let himself trust her. He'd never believe her love was freely given and he could never love her. Holding the check with both hands, she started to shake.

"This is very generous," she said in a deceptively

calm voice as she held back the pain. "But I can't help feeling you're hiding behind your money."

"You're wrong—"

"Don't tell me how to feel." Unless he could make her numb. "I was well paid for the work I did with Sean. And I care for him very much—" The lump of emotion in her throat grew and choked off the words.

Gavin ran his fingers through his hair. "I have the money. You need it. I'm just trying to help."

"You had that check ready when you showed up. You were planning to pick up Sean and give it to me. You never hand over money, no questions asked, unless you're paying someone to stay out of your life."

"No. I appreciate everything you did—"

"Including sleeping with you?" She felt brittle, breakable, and prayed she could hold herself together long enough to tell him what he could do with his help.

"It's not about that."

She believed him. The wanting was real and it scared him. It reinforced his decision to distance himself. He hadn't come here to make love to her and the fact that it had happened made this gesture all the more heartbreaking. If he could take a chance, the two of them could have had something special. "You can tell yourself this is a bonus, but what you're really doing is paying me off. Just like your father bought off your mother and you paid off Sean's."

"That's not fair." He put his hands on his hips as he glared at her.

"It's not about being fair. It's about facing the

truth. The truth is you just bought yourself an insurance policy with no deductible." She ripped the check in two. "And you got it for free." She ripped the halves again and again until she couldn't tear it anymore.

"M.J. listen to me—"

"There's nothing more I want to hear. I'm sure you've heard the saying. It's a cliché really. But I've never seen the truth of it more clearly than I do right now. Actions speak louder than words. And your actions are saying in a most articulate way exactly what you want."

"You've got it all wrong."

"I've got it right for the first time. You're afraid to care. You're afraid of not being in control." She met his gaze and prayed the threatening tears didn't show. "It should be comforting to know you won't fail at love. You can't fail at something you'll never try."

On her way out of the kitchen, she looked at the shreds of paper in her palm. Her heart felt just as torn apart. When she dropped the pieces in the trash, it hurt deep inside that Gavin had thrown away her love just as easily. She would never fail at love again, either.

Chapter Fifteen

M.J. rocked back and forth on the porch swing, breathing deeply of the heady scent of her mother's flowers. Bushes brimming with white, yellow, red and coral roses in between white and pink oleanders edged the expansive lawn. It was not too hot, not too cool, one of those perfect September days in California. Days like this usually made her feel cheerful, hopeful and just plain good.

Today? Not so much.

She'd substituted for a tenth-grade English teacher and it was late afternoon now. Referrals for speech therapy clients were starting to come in and balancing the two jobs would be challenging for a while.

But her financial problems were nothing more than an inconvenience compared to losing Gavin.

Correction—you couldn't lose something or someone you never had. It was clear she'd never had his regard and she felt like an idiot. She hated feeling that way, but she'd even take it over the soul-deep pain of knowing she would never see Gavin again. Or Sean. It had been a couple of weeks since the last time and the ache in her heart was getting worse instead of better. How would Gavin explain to his son that he couldn't come over anymore? How would Sean take it? She didn't want him to hurt. He'd been through so much. But she hoped he missed her a little.

The door beside her opened and her mother walked outside. "Here you are."

"Yup." M.J. smiled. She tried anyway. A feeble attempt to pretend she wasn't dying inside.

"Would you like some company?"

Not really, she wanted to say. She'd much prefer to be alone. Why spread this black-and-blue feeling around? It was bad enough her hopes and expectations had been drop-kicked down heartbreak highway. Inflicting this mood on unsuspecting optimists was just wrong.

"Doesn't Aunt Lil need help with dinner?"

Evelyn's mouth twisted wryly. "Let me pause and feel the welcoming warmth."

Ten seconds, M.J. thought. She couldn't hide the effects of her funk for ten lousy seconds.

"Sorry. I guess I'm not in a very good mood.

Don't get too close. I don't want you to catch it and bring you down to my level."

"I'll take my chances." Her mother sat beside her in the two-seater swing. "What's wrong, M.J.?"

It would be easier to tell her what wasn't wrong, so she decided not to talk about it at all. "Nothing."

"I'm your mom. I know something's bothering you."

M.J. slouched lower on the padded seat. "Guess I'm just tired."

"Bad day at school?"

Actually she'd had a pretty good day. She'd never been to that particular high school and the kids didn't know her. Surprisingly not one of the students in seven different classes had tested her authority. Maybe the scowl on her face and the make-my-day look in her eyes had made them think twice about pulling any antisocial antics.

"No." M.J. shook her head. "It was good."

"Then you're going to have to tell me what's wrong."

"But you're my mom." There was her inner snark acting up again. "I thought you knew."

"I know how to read your body language, smart aleck. Moping and remarks like that aren't difficult to decipher. But you're going to have to give me specifics."

"No, I—"

"Stop it. That's enough." It was the mom voice that brooked no disobedience. "Stop being a petulant child. You're feeling sorry for yourself and I want to know why. And before you try another excuse, let me say it's been particularly bad since Gavin was here. I simply want to help you."

M.J. had told Gavin that sometimes you need help cleaning up your mess. And the look on her mother's face said all she wanted to do was to make it better. Loving and protecting Sean had compelled M.J. to confront his father on his behalf.

M.J. had preached behavioral changes and breaking patterns to Gavin, albeit with marginal success in his personal relationships. But Sean was thriving in their newly formed boundaries. How could M.J. not take her own advice and meet her mother halfway? If she didn't, that would make her a "do as I say not as I do" person and she didn't want to be that way. All the pain, everything she'd been through would be for nothing if she didn't grab on to the hand her mother was holding out with love.

"Mom—" She sighed. "There's so much wrong, I don't even know where to start."

"How about the beginning?"

"You already know that part. What I left out was that Vince was a compulsive gambler and I'm paying off the enormous debt he left behind."

The words came out in a rush and M.J. waited for a reaction. She slid a sidelong glance at her frowning mother.

"A gambler?" Evelyn pulled her sweater tighter across her chest. "I know the two of you had your problems, but he seemed like a nice man."

"He was. And a good father," M.J. added.

She told her mother everything she'd told Gavin—about how Vince had managed to max out credit cards and hide what he was doing.

Somehow telling Gavin had helped her shed the bitterness and put things into clearer perspective. M.J. could remember without resentment now. Vince had loved his son. He'd also blamed himself for what happened to Brian. The crushing guilt fed his flaws and frailties. He'd never meant to hurt their son, it was careless, but it was an accident. In that moment M.J. realized she'd forgiven him. He was careless, not evil. And part of her heart would always hurt for the little boy they'd lost.

Now for the hard part. M.J. tucked her legs up and let her mother move the swing back and forth. "There's more, Mom, and it involves the house."

Evelyn went still, then slowly turned her head. "What?"

M.J. stared out at the land that had been in her family for so long. Land that she'd put in jeopardy. "He borrowed money against the house. I didn't know," she rushed on. "He forged my signature. After he died, it all came crashing down."

"On you," Evelyn said, her voice edged with anger.

"Every day there was a new crisis," M.J. confirmed. "A phone call demanding payment. A letter threatening legal action if an account wasn't brought current."

"That explains why you moved in with Lil and me. I thought it was about loneliness. About missing Brian."

"It was. Partly."

"I miss him, too."

M.J. folded her arms over her chest. "It's a mess."

"And little girls clean up after themselves," her mother said, clearly remembering their talk.

M.J. waited, but a long moment passed and she didn't say more. "Are you furious?"

"I am." Evelyn moved the swing, faster than before. "I'm furious on so many levels."

This was what M.J. had dreaded. Facing her mother, knowing she was a major disappointment. "Mom, I don't know what to say. I'm—"

"Don't say you're sorry. You didn't do anything wrong. I'm angry with Vince."

"I know." M.J. understood.

"I'm angry with you."

That was understandable, too. Except… "But you just said I didn't do anything…"

"You didn't cause the problem, but I can't help being angry that you didn't come to me."

"I was worried about your health. After the heart attack—"

Evelyn's fierce expression stopped her. "It was a mild attack. A warning, the doctor said. I've made lifestyle changes and there's no muscle damage. There's no apparent reason I can't live many healthy years. And I certainly don't need you to protect me."

"I thought it was the right thing, Mom."

"That's so like you. Trying to do the right thing." She reached out and covered M.J.'s hand with her own. "Mostly I'm angry with myself."

"For putting the house in my name," M.J. guessed.

"No. For giving you the impression that you had to deal with everything by yourself."

"Don't be angry. You didn't do anything wrong." M.J. turned her hand and linked fingers as she realized she'd just echoed her mother's words. "It's just that I love you so much. I was afraid if I wasn't good enough, you would leave me. Like my father did."

"He was a jerk." Evelyn sighed. "I love you more than anything in the world. It would never occur to me to abandon you. I can't imagine not being part of your life."

"You still feel that way? Even though the family home is vulnerable because of my husband?"

"Oh, please. I just wish you'd come to me when you found out you were pregnant. I suspected, but… I wish I'd said something." She shook her head. "When I found myself pregnant with you, there was a lot of family pressure. I was certainly mature enough to deal with it on my own, but everyone had an opinion. And times were different. People weren't as open-minded as they are now. I didn't want to influence you or tell you what to do with your own body." She sighed. "I just wish I'd let you know that I was there for you. That you didn't have to marry Vince, unless you loved him. If you hadn't made it legal…"

"The house wouldn't be in jeopardy," M.J. finished.

"That's not what I was going to say. We'll figure out what to do about that. Together," she said, squeezing M.J.'s fingers. The corners of her mouth curved up. "It occurs to me that we need to work on our communication."

"No kidding." M.J. smiled. "Although I think we just took a giant leap forward—" Her voice caught as emotion suddenly pulled tight in her chest. When she recovered a little, she said, "And I have to tell you, my heart feels lighter than it has since—"

"Since Gavin was here?"

"Actually, no. That was the day he handed my heart back to me in the form of a personal check."

"So you admit you're in love with Gavin?"

M.J. stretched her legs out and slouched in the swing. "Admitting it isn't really the problem. He can't love me back."

They talked for a long time—about Gavin's lonely childhood with a cold-hearted father. His disillusionment with the woman who'd bartered the life of a baby for money. His determination to get the best possible speech therapist for his son. M.J.'s heart felt lighter and yet heavier at the same time as she watched the sun slide behind the mountain, bathing the world in dusk.

Evelyn was quiet for a long time before she said, "Sweetie, it's very clear to me that Gavin wrote the check *because* he loves you and it scares the hell out of him."

Since when did her mother the realist live in a fantasy world? "Mom, have you ever been in love?"

"That's not the point. I—"

"What was it you just said about working on our communication?"

"All right. Yes. I was in love with your father. And I found out he didn't feel the same about me. But I still don't understand how he could turn his back on his bright, beautiful daughter. It was painful and I got over it."

"I'm sorry, Mom. You're right. If he could walk away from a wonderful woman like you, he was a jerk. Probably still is."

"Wherever he is." Evelyn laughed. "My point is that Gavin's not like your father. He needs you and he doesn't want to because he's learned not needing anyone doesn't hurt as much."

A breeze kicked up in the wake of the sun's disappearance. It was getting chilly and not just the air. M.J. felt cold all the way to her soul. She appreciated her mother's supportive words, however unhelpful they were. The damage was already done. She'd promised herself she wouldn't lose her heart to Sean and his father.

She'd broken that promise and the pain of it was setting in.

Through Sean she'd regained her professional life and taken the first steps in a new, wonderful relationship of communication and understanding with her mother. Sean was also the bridge to Gavin, who she knew was the love of her life. But she'd lost him before he was ever hers.

Now she would have to find a way to deal with the

behalf, it would remove any personal component. And if she'd accepted the check, she'd have fulfilled his low expectations. He could walk away without getting hurt.

He'd walked away, but his wounds were still open and raw. Now he realized there'd never been any way for him to get out unscathed. From the first day he'd met her, he'd thought he had it all figured out. But there was one thing he hadn't taken into consideration.

He hadn't counted on falling in love with her.

Sean walked across the sand and patted his thigh. "Daddy?"

Gavin glanced down. "Yeah, buddy?"

"You look sad."

Mad, sad, glad. Put your feelings into words. Was there anything he *hadn't* learned from M.J.?

Gavin was his son's role model. Children had a way of cutting through the crap and getting to the heart of the truth. If he wanted Sean to be honest with him, he had to show up for the hard stuff.

"I am sad." He went down on one knee and met his son's open, solemn gaze.

"Why?"

"Because—" How could he put this mess into terms this innocent child could understand? He cut right to the core. "I hurt her feelings."

Such an inadequate explanation of what he'd done.

"How, Daddy?"

Gavin had dreaded the question he knew was coming. How did he put into words the fact that he'd thrown her love back in her face? That he'd offered her money because he wanted control over feelings that were out of control. That she'd all but ordered him out of her house and certainly never wanted to see him again.

"How did you hurt her feelings, Daddy? Did you call her names?"

In his six-year-old frame of reference, Sean had nailed it. He'd called her names all right. Gold digger was at the top of the list.

Gavin looked into Sean's dark eyes. "Yeah, son. I kind of did call her a name."

The boy put his small hand on Gavin's shoulder. "Tell her you're sorry."

"I don't think that will help—"

"It will." The child nodded sagely. "M.J. says when you do something wrong, you always have to say you're sorry. It makes people feel better."

Not this time, Gavin thought. Sorry just wasn't enough to take away the deep hurt he'd seen in her expressive blue eyes. How could he not have realized that there wasn't a deceptive bone in her body? That she was sweet and giving and open and wouldn't know manipulation if it bit her in the backside? How could he have been so completely brainless?

Sean patted his shoulder. "You still look sad."

"Yeah."

"Sorry, Daddy."

Gavin's throat squeezed tight with emotion. He was awed and humbled by the simple wisdom of this child. His child. Gratitude swelled inside him for the miracle of a second chance with Sean. For the miracle of M.J. who had shown both of them how to appreciate each other and express their feelings.

Gavin knew he'd pushed the limit on miracles. He had no right to expect another one. And that's what it would take for M.J. to forgive him for the unforgivable.

This was a hell of a time to realize she'd been his one and only chance for happiness. He'd best get used to hell because he'd be living there from now on.

Chapter Sixteen

"What can we do to cheer you up?" Aunt Lil asked.

M.J. was aware that her aunt knew everything—about her husband's gambling problem, her debt, the mortgage.

And Gavin.

Her life was like the lyrics in a pathetic country-western song—if she didn't have a broken heart she'd have no heart at all.

Monday was chicken soup night and the three of them were cutting up vegetables and putting all the ingredients together. After that it would simmer for three hours until dinner. M.J. sighed as she looked at the big pot. All those "Chicken Soup" books for mind, soul, body or heart wouldn't help what ailed her. There was no advice or warm-and-fuzzy story that would take away her deep unhappiness. All she could do was try to hide her feelings better.

"I'm fine. Don't worry about me," she said.

Aunt Lil took the lid off the pot. "I know what might help."

Her mother looked up from the cutting board on the kitchen table. The piece of carrot she'd just sliced rolled away. "What?"

Aunt Lil put the whole chicken in the pot. "Let's have liquor."

Evelyn frowned. "It's too early. And it's Monday afternoon."

"I know what day and time it is." Her aunt frowned right back. "I also know M.J. doesn't have any more appointments today. Liquor would kind of shake things up."

Her mother looked skeptical. "Lil, do you really think M.J. needs more shaking up? Hasn't she been through enough?"

"What she needs is to get good and snockered, and tell Mr. Moneybags Gavin Spencer exactly what his problem is."

It wouldn't do any good to tell them she'd done that on more than one occasion and it hadn't made any difference. There was no reason to believe if she did it again that he could love her. Maybe if she hadn't spoken her mind there would be a chance, but she didn't think so. The whys didn't matter anymore. She looked at the two women—her family—and she loved them very much. That's when she realized the heart was a remarkable organ. If it weren't, she couldn't hurt about love and love so much at the same time.

M.J. put her arm around her aunt's shoulders. "I like the way you think, Aunt Lil. There's just one problem. I already told him off and it didn't make any difference."

"Did it make you feel better?" Lil asked.

"Yes," she lied.

"Then that's something. So, what do you say? Should I break out the cooking sherry?"

"I've tasted sherry and I have just one comment. Eww." M.J. wrinkled her nose and shuddered.

Lil shrugged and smiled. "It's the best I can do on such short notice."

M.J. kissed her aunt's soft, wrinkled cheek. "You're such a lightweight. And a fake."

She pointed her wooden spoon with mock severity. "I got a smile out of you, young lady."

With time, M.J. knew, the smiles would come without so much effort. Life went on and she'd go along with it. She'd been knocked around some, but she had a lot to be grateful for.

"Your aunt has always been the comic relief in the family." Evelyn picked up her cutting board and walked it over to the pot, then dumped the carrots in with the water and chicken. M.J. carried her plate of chopped onion and celery over and scraped it in.

"You're also a fabulous cook, Aunt Lil. A woman of many talents."

"I'm also sexy and mysterious," she said with a twinkle in her eyes.

"That goes without saying. I think—" The doorbell rang, interrupting the words.

As M.J. walked to the door, her heart beat faster because her last unexpected visitor had been Gavin Spencer. It wasn't likely to be him and the thought brought a fresh wave of pain. Would she ever stop thinking about him and hurting?

M.J. opened the door and saw a Spencer, but it wasn't Gavin. "Sean!"

"Hi."

"Hi. Sweetie, what are you doing here?"

"I wanted to come Saturday."

Her heart caught. She'd missed him terribly. "It's good to see you, but—"

The familiar car idling on the drive in front of the house pulled away. The windows were tinted but she was pretty sure Henderson was behind the wheel. He'd waited to make sure Sean made his connection before leaving.

She put a hand on her hip. "Was that Henderson?"

Sean nodded. "Daddy told him he could bring me anytime I wanted to come."

It would have been better if he'd called before just dropping the boy off, but probably Henderson figured Gavin had handled that. And it was unlikely that Gavin discussed personal issues with his staff so they had no idea things had changed. Which meant...

M.J. went down on one knee and took the boy's hands. "Sweetie, does your dad know you're here?"

He stared at her for a long moment and then shook his head. "No."

"Oh, Sean, you probably shouldn't have come without his permission."

"But I had to. I wanted to see you and Auntie Ev and Aunt Lil." His eyes were bleak.

"And we want to see you, too. You're always welcome here, but you should have checked with your dad first."

"Daddy's sad."

That made two of them and M.J. figured she was going to hell for being glad she wasn't the only one. But what was Gavin's excuse?

"I'm sorry your dad is sad, but—"

"Me, too." He rubbed a finger under his nose. "I told him I was sorry even though I didn't do nothin'—"

"Anything," she automatically corrected.

"Anything bad. You always telled—" He stopped and thought about that. "Told me to say sorry."

"Yes." She brushed the dark hair off his forehead. She'd missed this child. He was a very sweet, smart, special little boy. He was a Spencer.

"But, M.J." Confusion swirled in his dark eyes. "It didn't help. Daddy's still sad. He said he hurt your feelings and kind of called you a bad name."

"I see."

"I told him to say sorry, but he said it wouldn't help this time." His gaze filled with pleading. "I told him you always say try your best, but he still looked sad."

Wow. Gavin was really getting into the communication thing with his son. It also sounded like he was getting that he'd been a super jerk, but she couldn't afford to go there. Hope was a terrible thing to waste.

And this wasn't about her. Gavin would be frantic if he couldn't find his son.

She stood and held out her hand. "Come inside, sweetie. I'm going to call your dad before he gets worried."

Sean nodded, then put his little hand in hers and let her lead him inside.

M.J. was pacing the living room when Gavin knocked softly on the door. The sound made her jump and it wasn't as if she hadn't been expecting him. When she'd called him on his cell and explained what happened, he'd said he would be right over. Her nerves were stretched to the snapping point and she wanted this meeting over.

Her chest felt tight and it took several deep breaths to relieve the pressure.

She braced herself before opening the door. And there he was, looking really good, every inch the rumpled and busy CEO. She braced herself again before saying, "Hello, Gavin."

"M.J." He glanced inside. "Where's Sean?"

"In the attic with my mother." She started to turn away. "I'll get him—"

"Wait," he said, reaching out a hand to stop her.

His fingers were warm on her wrist and brought back painful reminders of how good it felt when he touched her, followed by aching sadness for what could never be. She didn't want to wait. She wanted him to go before she couldn't hide what seeing him was doing to her. When she looked into his eyes, then at his hand, he removed it.

"What?" she asked, folding her arms over her chest as she stood in the doorway.

"How are you?"

"Fine."

"Really?"

"Of course."

"You look tired," he said.

"Thank you." Why was he doing this? Pretending he actually cared was ripping her heart out.

"Are you still working two jobs?"

"What do you care?"

"How's it going?" he asked, not answering the question.

She knew what he was asking and if answers would get him out of here sooner, she'd give them to him. "Mom knows everything."

"How did she take it?"

"Surprisingly well," she admitted. "She's going to work part-time at a nursery not far from here. She loves plants and figures it will be good for her. She starts at the end of the week."

"So you're not dealing with all of it by yourself. I'm glad."

So was she. And in a way Gavin was responsible. He'd listened and made changes at her suggestion. She'd decided he was right about sharing the burden.

"We're also thinking of taking in boarders. College kids maybe. This house is so big and has a couple of extra bedrooms and baths. That was Aunt Lil's idea."

"It's a good one."

She stuck her fingers in the pockets of her jeans. "We're family. Families pull together and help each other." She'd also learned that no one could help if you kept secrets.

"Speaking of helping—"

Her stomach knotted. "Don't go there, Gavin. I don't want or need your kind of help."

"I wasn't going to offer. The last time—" He ran his fingers through his hair. "It was a stupid, clumsy thing to do."

"I couldn't have said it better. And I couldn't agree more. I'll get Sean now—"

"I'm not finished."

"What else is there to say?"

"Plenty." But doubts darkened his eyes to almost black. "I've made a complete mess of things, M.J. You were right about everything you said when I gave you that check."

She remembered the pain and heartbreak represented in that piece of paper. "I didn't want or need it."

"I know that now. But I need you, M.J."

Now she was just shocked. "You do?"

He nodded. "But I didn't want to need you because everyone I ever needed left me and I believed you would, too. I told myself I was being noble, helping you out of a jam. So I offered you money. I was the good guy. So when you walked, it wasn't my failure."

She looked into his eyes, bleak and troubled, so like his son's. Pain squeezed inside her, but not for herself this time. She ached for Gavin, for his lost childhood and the cruelty of the impossible standard his father imposed on him.

She touched his arm. "It's all right, Gavin."

"No." He shook his head, misery etched on his chiseled features. "It was unforgivable. You shouldn't hurt the ones you love."

"Love?"

"Yeah." He laughed bitterly. "Isn't that ironic? I've ruined everything with you and it's the worst failure of my life. Because you're the love of my life."

Hope exploded inside her like the fireworks finale on the Fourth of July. "You love me?"

"Yeah." His gaze locked with hers. "I've never been more scared than when Sean got hurt. But they say every cloud has a silver lining. And you're mine."

"I'm your cliché? Am I supposed to think that's a good thing?"

"Definitely. I found you and requested that you work with Sean—"

"Requested? Excuse me. Harassed would be a more accurate description," she said.

His smile was fleeting. "The truth is, M.J., you taught my son how to use language again. At the same time you taught me how to love."

"I did?" She was awed and humbled by what he was telling her. She believed him. Because of the tormented look on his face. Because actions speak louder than words and there was no check in his hand. He was telling her he loved her without any reason to trust she wouldn't reject him. And her heart swelled with love for this good and decent man.

"You did. And the lesson is priceless—something money can't buy."

"Oh, Gavin—" Emotion choked off her words.

He took her hands in his. "I love you, M.J. I'm so sorry I hurt you. The thing is, I found out everything is useless without you. At least, it feels that way. Sean feels it, too. I know you never wanted to see me again, but I'm glad I got the chance to tell you how much I'll always regret being a jerk. I'll get Sean and—"

"Don't you want to know how I feel?"

"Of course. I just didn't think you'd be able to stand the sight of me—"

She put a finger on his mouth to stop him. "I need to thank you for something, too. You single-handedly dragged me kicking and screaming from the place where I was hiding. I'll always love and miss my son, but not using the skills I've learned to help children is a disservice to his memory. How can I not love the man who made me see that?"

He blinked. "You love me?"

"Yes. I'm in love with you, Gavin Spencer."

"And I'm in love with you, Mary Jane Taylor."

They smiled at each other for several moments before he tugged her into his arms and kissed her for a very long time. When he finally pulled away and gulped in air, he rested his forehead against hers.

"I have a request," he said.

"Another one?" She pulled back and looked into his eyes, clear and dark and free of doubt.

"I respectfully request that you be my wife and Sean's mother. Marry me, M.J."

"Nothing would make me happier."

The sound of footsteps on the stairs made them turn. Sean stood at the bottom of the steps, taking in the sight of them in each other's arms. He looked at his father. "Daddy, you don't look sad anymore."

"I'm not. How would you feel about M.J. living with us forever?"

The child grinned and held up his hand. "High five, Daddy."

Gavin gave him a high five. "So it's okay with you that she's going to marry me?"

Sean nodded enthusiastically. "I love M.J."

"I love you, too, Sean." She pulled him close to them. "Group hug. Family hug."

Gavin met her gaze. "I don't deserve to be this

happy. But I'm extremely grateful that you agreed to be my wife."

M.J. smiled at the two Spencer men—her men. She understood how Gavin felt and figured questioning their good fortune was a waste of precious time.

At her millionaire's request, she would spend her time simply loving her family.

* * * * *

Page-turning drama…

Exotic, glamorous locations…

Intense emotion and passionate seduction…

Sheikhs, princes and billionaire tycoons…

This summer, may we suggest:

THE SHEIKH'S DISOBEDIENT BRIDE
by Jane Porter
On sale June.

AT THE GREEK TYCOON'S BIDDING
by Cathy Williams
On sale July.

THE ITALIAN MILLIONAIRE'S VIRGIN WIFE
On sale August.

With new titles to choose from every month,
discover a world of romance in our books written
by internationally bestselling authors.

HARLEQUIN *Presents*

It's the ultimate in quality romance!

Available wherever Harlequin books are sold.

www.eHarlequin.com   HPGEN06

**Hidden in the secrets of antiquity,
lies the unimagined truth...**

Introducing

a brand-new line filled with mystery
and suspense, action and adventure,
and a fascinating look into history.

And it all begins with DESTINY.

In a sealed crypt in
France, where the
terrifying legend of
the beast of Gevaudan
begins to unravel,
Annja Creed discovers
a stunning artifact
that will seal her destiny.

*Available every other
month starting
July 2006, wherever
you buy books.*

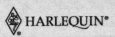

Stability is highly overrated….

Dana Logan's world had always revolved around her children. Now they're all grown up and don't seem to need anything she's able to give them. Struggling to find her new identity, Dana realizes that it's about time for her to get "off her rocker" and begin a new life!

Off Her Rocker

by Jennifer Archer

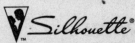

COMING NEXT MONTH

#1771 BACK IN THE BACHELOR'S ARMS—Victoria Pade
Northbridge Nuptials
Years ago, when Chloe Carmichael was pregnant by high school sweetheart Reid Walker, her meddling parents sent her out of town and told Reid she'd lost the baby. Now Chloe was back to sell her parents' old house—and *Dr.* Reid Walker was the buyer. Soon he discovered the child he never knew…and rediscovered the woman he'd never forgotten.

#1772 FINDING NICK—Janis Reams Hudson
Tribute, Texas
Shannon Malloy's book about 9/11 heroes was almost done—but when she tracked her last interview subject, injured New York firefighter Nick Carlucci, to Tribute, Texas, he wasn't talking. While Nick denied Shannon access to his story, he couldn't deny her access to his heart—especially when he realized their shared connection to the tragedy….

#1773 THE PERFECT WIFE—Judy Duarte
Talk of the Neighborhood
Rich, thin Carly Anderson had a fairy-tale life…until her husband left her for her friend down the street. Carly became reclusive—maybe even chubby!—but when worried neighbors coaxed her out to the local pool, she was pleasantly surprised to meet carpenter Bo Conway. Would this down-to-earth man help Carly get to *happily ever after* after all?

#1774 OUTBACK BABY—Lilian Darcy
Wanted: Outback Wives
City girl Shay Russell had come to the Australian Outback in flood season to rethink her values. And when she dropped into cattleman Dusty Tanner's well-ordered life after a helicopter crash, two worlds literally collided. Soon, not only the waters, but the passions, were running high on the Outback….until Shay told Dusty she was pregnant.

#1775 THE PRODIGAL M.D. RETURNS—Marie Ferrarella
The Alaskans
Things really heated up in Hades, Alaska, when skirt-chasing Ben Kerrigan came back to town. But after leaving Heather Ryan Kendall at the altar seven years ago, Dr. Ben was a reformed man. Soon Ben was back paying Heather personal house calls…but recently widowed Heather and her six-year-old daughter had a surprise for the prodigal M.D.

#1776 JESSIE'S CHILD—Lois Faye Dyer
The McClouds of Montana
Even a decades-old family feud couldn't stop Jessie McCloud and Zack Kerrigan from sharing a night of passion—just one night. But four years later, when Zack returned from military duty overseas, he discovered that *just one night* had had lifelong consequences. Could Jessie and Zack overcome dueling family traditions to raise their son…together?

SSECNM0706